D1605555

Blue Christmas and Other Holiday Homicides

Other Five Star Titles
by Max Allan Collins:

Butcher's Dozen
Mourn the Living

Blue Christmas and Other Holiday Homicides

Max Allan Collins

Five Star • Waterville, Maine

Five Star First Edition Mystery Series.

Published in 2001 in conjunction with Tekno-Books and Ed Gorman.

Set in 11 pt. Plantin by Al Chase.

Printed in the United States on permanent paper.

Library of Congress Cataloging-in-Publication Data

Collins, Max Allan.
    Blue Christmas and other holiday homicides / Max Allan Collins.—[1st ed.]
        p.   cm.—(Five Star first edition mystery series)
    Contents: A wreath for Marley—Mommy—Flowers for Bill Reilly—His father's ghost—Firecracker kill—A bird for Becky.
    ISBN 0-7862-3551-9 (hc : alk. paper)
    1. Detective and mystery stories, American.
2. Christmas stories, American.   I. Title: Blue Christmas.
II. Title.   III. Series.
PS3553.O4753 B58 2001
813'.54—dc21   2001040253

For Marty and Ed

Table of Contents

Blue Christmas—An Introduction   7

CHRISTMAS: A Wreath for Marley   11

MOTHER'S DAY: Mommy   51

MEMORIAL DAY: Flowers for Bill O'Reilly   78

FATHER'S DAY: His Father's Ghost   105

FOURTH OF JULY: Firecracker Kill   129

THANKSGIVING: A Bird for Becky   164

Blue Christmas

—An Introduction

The title of this book is an alternate title for the lead story herein, "A Wreath for Marley." This particular short story—a novella, really—is probably my favorite piece of fiction I ever wrote. I didn't say it was the best thing I ever wrote—though I admit to thinking it's pretty good—just my favorite. Here's why.

In 1992, the day before Thanksgiving, I was—without warning, and well after my contractual option had kicked in—informed by letter that I was no longer wanted by the *Chicago Tribune Syndicate* to write the *Dick Tracy* comic strip. Though this was not entirely without warning—I'd had an extremely bad relationship with the syndicate's new editor, who'd replaced the man who hired me in 1977—the news was nonetheless a shock. The consensus was that I had revitalized the strip, and I'd been involved with the recent movie, consulting with the producers, writing a best-selling novelization, as well as a series of *Tracy* novels. I was developing several other *Tracy* projects for Tribune Media Services—including a series of juvenile novels—and had reason to believe my job was secure.

The same day that letter arrived, I also learned that my contract with Bantam Books to write several more of my Nathan Heller novels had been—with no warning whatsoever—dropped. A few weeks before, the most recent Heller—*Stolen Away*—had won the Shamus Award for best novel; and

7

I'd spent a three-hour luncheon with my Bantam editor, during which she had outlined a rosy future for Heller and me (may coal forever find its way to her stocking).

The 1992 holidays were, potentially, bleak indeed. The *Chicago Tribune Syndicate*—firing me after fifteen years of helming *Tracy*—really knew how to set the stage for a great Thanksgiving and Christmas; and Bantam Books wasn't bad at playing Scrooge, either.

One thing that saved my sanity—and helped ease my family's uncertainty—was an act of kindness by my friends Marty Greenberg and Ed Gorman. Learning of my plight— arch word, "plight," but accurate—Marty and Ed threw every short story assignment at me they possibly could. They kept me alive, financially, for about six months, and also allowed me to maintain my self-respect as a professional writer.

The other thing was "A Wreath for Marley," a.k.a. "Blue Christmas." I have always loved *A Christmas Carol*; it's my favorite Dickens yarn, and my wife and I watch the 1951 Alastair Sim film version every year, a ritual of enjoyment. On the weekend following Christmas 1992, I wrote "A Wreath for Marley"—the manuscript was 50 pages—in one sitting. It's my personal record for one sustained white-heat blast of work . . . I believe I finished at dawn, having started in the mid-evening.

I thought it was a terrific story—and I still do—and a great idea, combining *The Maltese Falcon* and the Dickens classic. (Modernizations of the Scrooge tale always seem to retain the stinginess of the main character and simply update the tale; my idea was to do a completely different story—with a protagonist who had his own set of frailties— but use the same structure . . . *another* Christmas carol.) But what was most important about the experience was the self-confidence—the exhilaration of being able to write for the sheer joy of it—that "Marley" had given me.

It was a hell of a gift.

The story didn't sell immediately. *Ellery Queen*'s editor, though expressing a liking for the tale, turned "Marley" down because of its length; but an anthology took it shortly after that. A few years ago I wrote a screenplay version, which I hope to direct and produce myself, one day (it is called "Blue Christmas"). I also published two sequels about "Marley" protagonist, Richard Stone—"A Bird for Becky" and "Flowers for Bill O'Reilly"—which also focused on holidays.

These three stories form a sort of spine for this collection, fleshed out with other holiday stories that I've done over the years. Not every holiday is represented here, and there may be further Richard Stone tales—and holiday homicides—in the future. I begin with Christmas, and end with Thanksgiving, and have arranged the tales between to follow the calendar, accordingly. ("Flowers for Bill O'Reilly," however, actually comes chronologically after "A Bird for Becky"; but for this volume's purposes, the arrangement I've chosen seems to flow better.)

Several thank yous are necessary. Marty and Ed, of course; my wife Barb and son Nathan, who saw me through that memorable holiday season of '92; and my actor pal Mike Cornelison, who co-wrote with me a screen treatment from which "Firecracker Kill" in part derives. Some of you may be familiar with my independent film "Mommy," which also exists in novel form (a sequel, "Mommy's Day," is both a novel and film); but the short story in this collection is where the Mommy saga began.

Though these holiday tales all involve homicide in one form or another, I hope the opening and closing novellas—"A Wreath for Marley" and "A Bird for Becky"—leave you with warm thoughts and happy memories of holiday seasons past. For me, the package of Christmas is tied up in ribbons of wonderful stories—miracles on 34th Street, various Scrooges (particularly Alastair Sim!) and Red Ryder beebee guns, courtesy of the late Jean Shepherd. If some of you add "A Wreath for Marley" to your personal list of seasonal favorites, that would be the best gift I could ever hope to receive.

CHRISTMAS

A Wreath for Marley

Private detective Richard Stone wasn't much for celebrations, or holidays—or holiday celebrations, for that matter.

Nonetheless, this Christmas Eve, in the year of our Lord 1942, he decided to throw a little holiday party in the modest two-room suite of offices on Wabash that he had once shared with his late partner, Jake Marley.

Present for the festivities were his sandy-tressed cutie-pie secretary, Katie Crockett, and his fresh-faced young partner, Joey Ernest. Last to arrive was his best pal (at least since Jake died), burly homicide dick Sgt. Hank Ross.

Katie had strung up some tinsel and decorated a little tree by her reception desk. Right now the little group was having a Yuletide toast with heavily rum-spiked eggnog. The darkly handsome Stone's spirits were good—just this morning, he'd been declared 4-F, thanks to his flat feet.

"Every flatfoot should have 'em!" he laughed.

"What'd you do?" Ross asked. "Bribe the draft-board doc?"

"What's it to you?" Stone grinned. "You cops get automatic deferments!"

And the two men clinked cups.

Actually, bribing the draft-board doctor was exactly what Stone had done; but he saw no need mentioning it.

"Hell," Joey said—and the word was quite a curse coming

11

from this kid, "I wish I *could* go. If it wasn't for this damn perforated eardrum . . ."

"You and Sinatra," Stone laughed.

Katie said nothing; her eyes were on the framed picture on her desk—her young brother Ben, who was spending Christmas in the Pacific somewhere.

"I got presents for all of you," Stone said, handing envelopes around.

"What's this?" Joey asked, confused, opening his envelope to see a slip of paper with a name and address on the South Side.

"Best black market butcher in the city," Stone said. "You and the missus and the brood can start the next year out with a coupla sirloins, on me."

"I'd feel funny about that . . . it's not legal . . ."

"Jesus! How can you be such a square and still work for me? You're lucky there's a man-power shortage, kid."

Ross, envelope open, was thumbing through five twenty-dollar bills. "You always know just what to get me, Stoney."

"Cops are so easy to shop for," Stone said.

Katie, seeming embarrassed, whispered her thanks into Stone's ear.

"Think nothin' of it, baby," he said. "It's as much for me as for you."

He'd given her a fifty-dollar gift certificate at the lingerie counter at Marshall Field's. Not every boss would be so generous.

They all had gifts for him, too: Joey gave him a $10 war bond, Katie a hand-tooled leather shoulder holster, and Hank the latest *Esquire* "Varga" calendar.

"To give this rat-trap some class," the cop said.

Joey raised his cup. "Here's to Mr. Marley," he said.

"To Mr. Marley," Katie said, her eyes suddenly moist. "Rest his soul."

"Yeah," Ross said, lifting his cup, "here's to Jake—dead a year to the day."

"To the night, actually," Stone said, and hoisted his cup. "What the hell—to my partner Jake. You were a miserable bastard, but Merry Christmas, anyway."

"You shouldn't talk that way!" Katie said.

"Even if it's the truth?" Stone asked with a smirk.

Suddenly it got quiet.

Then Ross asked, "Doesn't it bother you, Stoney? You're a detective and your partner's murder goes unsolved? Ain't it bad for business?"

"Naw. Not when you do mostly divorce work."

Ross grinned, shook his head. "Stoney, you're an example to us all," he said, waved, and ambled out.

Katie had a heartsick expression. "Doesn't Mr. Marley's death mean *anything* to you? He was your best friend!"

Stone patted his .38 under his shoulder. "Sadie here's my best friend. And, sure, Marley's death means something to me: full ownership of the business, and the only name on the door is mine."

She shook her head, slowly, sadly. "I'm so disappointed in you, Richard . . ."

He took her gently aside. "Then I'm not welcome at your apartment anymore?" he whispered.

"Of course you're welcome. I'm still hoping you'll come have Christmas dinner with my family and me, tomorrow."

"I'm not much for family gatherings. Ain't it enough I got you the black-market turkey?"

"Richard!" She shushed him. "Joey will hear . . ."

"What, and find out you're no Saint Kate?" He gave her a smack of a kiss on the forehead, then patted her fanny. "See you the day after . . . we'll give that new casino on Rush Street a try."

She sighed, said, "Merry Christmas, Richard," gathered her coat and purse, and went out.

Now it was just Joey and Stone. The younger man said, "You know, Katie's starting to get suspicious."

"About what?"

"About what. About you and Mrs. Marley!"

Stone snorted. "Katie just thinks I'm bein' nice to my late partner's widow."

"You being 'nice' is part of why it seems so suspicious. While you were out today, Mrs. Marley called about five times."

"The hell! Katie didn't say so."

"See what I mean?" Joey plucked his topcoat off the coat tree. "Mr. Stone—please don't expect me to keep covering for you. It makes me feel . . . dirty."

"Are you *sure* you were born in Chicago, kid?" Stone opened the door for him. "Go home! Have yourself a merry the hell little Christmas! Tell your kids Santa's comin', send 'em up to bed, and make the missus under the mistletoe one time for me."

"Thanks for the sentiment, Mr. Stone," he said, and was gone.

Stone—alone, now—decided to skip the eggnog and head straight for the rum. He was downing a cup when a knock called him to the door.

Two representatives of the Salvation Army stepped into his outer office, in uniform—a white-haired old gent, with a charity bucket, and a pretty shapely thing, her innocent face devoid of make-up under the Salvation Army bonnet.

"We're stopping by some of the offices to—" the old man began.

14

"Make a touch," Stone finished. "Sure thing. Help yourself to the eggnog, pops." Then he cast a warm smile on the young woman. "Honey, step inside my private office . . . that's where I keep the cash."

He shut himself and the little dame inside his office and got a twenty-dollar bill out of his cashbox from a desk drawer, then tucked the bill inside the swell of the girl's blouse.

Her eyes widened. "Please!"

"Baby, you don't have to say 'please.' " Stone put his hands on her waist and brought her to him. "Come on . . . give Santa a kiss."

Her slap sounded like a gunshot, and stung like hell. He whisked the bill back out of her blouse.

"Some Christmas spirit *you* got," he said, and opened the door and pushed her into the outer office.

"What's the meaning of this?" the old man sputtered, and Stone wadded up the twenty, tossed it in the bucket and shoved them both out the door.

"Squares," he muttered, returning to his rum.

Before long, the door opened and a woman in black appeared there, like a curvaceous wraith. Her hair was icy blonde, her thin lips blood red, like cuts in her angular white Joan Crawford-ish face. It had been a while since she'd seen forty, but she was better preserved than your grandma's strawberry jam.

She fell immediately into his arms. "Merry Christmas, darling!"

"In a rat's ass," he said coldly, pushing her away.

"Darling . . . what's wrong . . . ?"

"You been calling the office again! I told you not to do that. People are gonna get the wrong idea."

He'd been through this with her a million times: they were perfect suspects for Jake Marley's murder; neither of them had an alibi for the time of the killing—Stone was in his apartment, alone, and Maggie claimed she'd been alone at home, too.

But to cover for each other, they had lied to the cops about being together at Marley's penthouse, waiting for his return for a Christmas Eve supper.

"If people think we're an item," Stone told her, "we'll be prime suspects!"

"It's been a year . . ."

"That's not long enough."

She threw her head back and her blonde hair shimmered, and so did her diamond earrings. "I want to get out of black, and be on your arm, unashamed . . ."

"Since when were you ever ashamed of anything?" He shuddered, wishing he'd never met Maggie Marley, let alone climbed in bed with her; now, he was in bed with her, for God knew how long, and in every sense of the word. . . .

She touched his face with a gloved hand. "Are we spending Christmas Eve together, Richard?"

"Can't, baby. Gotta spend it with relatives."

"Who, your uncle and aunt?" She smirked in disbelief. "I can't believe you're going back to *farm* country, to see them . . . You *hate* it there!"

"Hey, wouldn't be right not seein' 'em. Christmas and all."

Her gaze seemed troubled. "I'd hoped we could talk. Richard . . . we may have a problem . . ."

"Such as?"

". . . Eddie's trying to blackmail me."

"Eddie? What does that slimy little bastard want?"

Eddie was Jake Marley's brother.

"He's in over his head with the Outfit," she said.

"What, gambling losses again? He'll never learn . . ."

16

"He's trying to squeeze me for dough," she said urgently. "He's got photos of us, together . . . at that resort!"

"So what?" he shrugged.

"Photos of us in *our* room at that resort . . . and he's got the guest register."

Stone frowned. "That was just a week after Jake was killed."

"I know. You were . . . consoling me."

Who was she trying to kid?

Stone said, "I'll talk to him."

She moved close to him again. "He's waiting for me now, at the Blue Spot Bar . . . would you keep the appointment for me, Richard?"

And she kissed him. Nobody kissed hotter than this dame. Or colder . . .

Half an hour later, Stone entered the smoky Rush Street saloon, where a thrush in a gown cut to her toenails was embracing the microphone, singing "White Christmas" off-key.

He found mustached weasel Eddie Marley sitting at the bar working on a Scotch—a bald little man in a bow tie and a plaid zoot suit.

"Hey, Dickie . . . nice to see ya. Buy ya a snort?"

"Don't call me 'Dickie.' "

"Stoney, then."

"Grab your topcoat and let's talk in my office," Stone said, nodding toward the alley door.

A cat chasing a rat made garbage cans clatter as the two men came out into the alley. A cold Christmas rain was falling, puddling on the frozen remains of a snow and ice storm from a week before. Ducking into the recession of a doorway, Eddie got out a cigarette and Stone, a statue standing out in the rain, leaned in with a Zippo to light it for him.

17

For a moment, the world wasn't pitch dark. But only for a moment.

"I don't *like* to stick it to ya, Stoney . . . but if I don't cough up five gees to the Outfit, I won't live to see '43! My brother left me high and dry, ya know."

"I'm all choked up, Eddie."

Eddie was shrugging. "Jake's life insurance paid off big—double indemnity. So Maggie's sittin' pretty. And the agency partnership reverted to you—so you're in the gravy. Where's that leave Eddie?"

Stone picked him up by the throat. The little man's eyes opened wide and his cigarette tumbled from his lips and sizzled in a puddle.

"It leaves you on your ass, Eddie."

And the detective hurled the little man into the alley, onto the pavement, where he bounced up against some garbage cans.

"Ya shouldn'ta done that, ya bastid! I got the goods on ya!"

Stone's footsteps splashed toward the little man. "You got nothin', Eddie."

"I got photos! I got your handwritin' on a motel register!"

"Don't try to tell *me* the bedroom-dick business. You bring me the negatives and the register page, and I'll give you five C's. First and last payment."

The weasel's eyes went very wide. "Five C's?!? I need five *G*'s by tomorrow—they'll break my knees if I don't pay up! Have a heart—have some Christmas charity, fer chrissakes!"

Stone pulled his trenchcoat collars up around his face. "I gave at the office, Eddie. Five C's is all you get."

"What are ya—Scrooge? Maggie's rich! And you're rolling in your own dough!"

Stone kicked Eddie in the side and the little man howled.

"The negatives and the register page, Eddie. Hit me up again and you'll take a permanent swim in the Chicago River. Agreed?"

"Agreed! Don't hurt me anymore! *Agreed!*"

"Merry X-mas, moron," Stone said, and exited the alley, pausing near the street to light up his own cigarette. Christmas carols were being piped through department store loud speakers: *"Joy to the world!"*

"In a rat's ass," he muttered, and hailed a taxi. In the back seat, he sipped rum from a flask. The cabbie made holiday small talk and Stone said, "Make you a deal—skip the chatter and maybe you'll get a tip for Christmas."

Inside his Gold Coast apartment building, Stone was waiting for the elevator when he caught a strange reflection in a lobby mirror. He saw—or *thought* he saw—an imposing trenchcoated figure in a fedora standing behind him.

His late partner—Jake Marley!

Stone whirled, but . . . no one was there.

He blew out air, glanced at the mirror again, seeing only himself. "No more rum for you, pal."

On the seventh floor, Stone unlocked 714 and slipped inside his apartment. The *art moderne* furnishings reflected his financial success; the divorce racket had made him damn near wealthy. He tossed his jacket on a half-circle white couch, loosened his tie and headed to his well-appointed bar, already changing his mind about more rum.

He'd been lying, of course, about going to see his uncle and aunt. Christmas out in the sticks—*that* was a laugh! That had just been an excuse, so he didn't have to spend the night with that blood-sucking Maggie.

From the icebox he built a salami and Swiss cheese on rye, smearing on hot mustard. Drifting back into the living room, where only one small lamp was on, he switched on his console radio, searching for sports or swing music or even war news, anything other than damn Christmas carols. But that maudlin muck was all he could find, and he switched it off in disgust.

Settling in a comfy overstuffed chair, still in his shoulder holster, he sat and ate and drank. Boredom crept in on him like ground fog.

Katie was busy with family tonight, and even most of the hookers he knew were taking the night off.

What the hell, he thought. *I'll just enjoy my own good company . . .*

Without realizing it, he drifted off to sleep; a noise woke him, and Sadie—his trusty .38—was in his hand before his eyes had opened all the way.

"Who's there?" he said, and stood. Somebody had switched off the lamp! *Who in hell?* The room was in near darkness. . . .

"Sorry, keed," a familiar voice said. "The light hurts my peepers."

Standing by the window was his late partner—Jake Marley.

"I must be dreamin'," Stone said rationally, after just the briefest flinch of a reaction, " 'cause, pal—you're dead as a doornail."

"I'm dead, all right," Marley said. "Been dead a whole year." Red neon, from the window behind him, pulsed in on the tall, trenchcoated fedora-sporting figure—a hawkishly handsome man with a grooved face and thin mustache. "But, keed—you ain't dreamin'."

"What sorta gag *is* this . . . ?"

Stone walked over to Marley and took a close look: no make-up, no mask—it was no masquerade. And the trenchcoat had four scorched holes stitched across the front.

Bullet holes.

He put a hand on Marley's shoulder—and it passed right through.

"Jesus!" Stone stepped back. "You're not dead—I'm dead *drunk*." He turned away. "Havin' the heebie-jeebies or somethin'. When I wake up, you better be gone, or I'm callin' Ripley . . ."

Marley smiled a little. "Nobody can see me but you, keed. Talk about it, and they'll toss ya in the laughin' academy, and throw away the key. Mind if I siddown? Feet are killin' me."

"Your eyes hurt, your feet hurt—what kinda goddamn ghost *are* you, anyway?"

" 'Zactly what you said, keed," Marley said, and he slowly moved toward the sofa, dragging himself along, to the sound of metallic scraping. "The God-*damned* kind . . . and I'll stay that way if you don't come through for me."

Below the trenchcoat, Marley's feet were heavily shackled, like a chain-gang prisoner.

"You think *mine's* heavy," Marley said, "wait'll ya see what the boys in the metal shop are cookin' up for you."

The ghost sat heavily, his shackles clanking. Stone kept his distance.

"What do ya want from me, Jake?"

"The near-impossible, keed—I want ya to do the right thing."

"The right thing?"

"Find my murderer, ya chowderhead! Jesus!" At that last exclamation, Marley cowered, glanced upward, muttering, "No offense, Boss," and continued: "You're a detective, Stoney—when a detective's partner's killed, he's supposed to do somethin' about it. That's the code."

"That's the bunk," Stone said. "I left it to the cops. They mucked it up." He shrugged. "End of story."

"Nooooo!" Marley moaned, sounding like a ghost for the

21

first time, and making the hair stand up on Stone's neck. "I was your partner, I was your only friend . . . your *mentor* . . . and you let me die an unsolved murder while you took over my business—*and* my wife."

Stone flinched again; lighted up a Lucky. "You know about that, huh? Maggie, I mean."

"Of course I know!" Marley waved a dismissive hand. "Oh, her I don't care two cents about . . . she always was a witch, with a capital 'b.' Having her in your life is punishment enough for *any* crime. But, keed—you and me, we're *tied* to each other! Chained for eternity. . . ."

Convinced he was dreaming, Stone snorted. "Really, Jake? How come?"

Marley leaned forward and his shackles clanked. "My best pal—a detective—didn't think I was worth a measly murder investigation. Where I come from, a man who can't inspire any more loyalty than *that* outa his best pal is one lost soul."

Stone shrugged. "It was nothin' personal."

"Oh, I take gettin' murdered *real* personal! And you didn't give a rat's ass *who* killed me! And that's why *you're* as good as damned."

"Baloney!" Stone touched his stomach. ". . . or maybe salami . . ."

Marley shifted in his seat and his shackles rattled. "You *knew* I always looked after my little brother, Eddie—he's a louse and weakling, but he was the only brother I had . . . and what have you done for Eddie? Tossed him in some garbage cans! Left 'im for the Boys to measure for cement overshoes!"

"He's a weasel."

"He's your dead best pal's brother! Cut him some slack!"

"I did cut him some slack! I didn't kill him when he tried to blackmail me."

"Over you sleeping with his dead brother's wife, you mean?"

Stone batted the air dismissively. "The hell with you, Marley! You're not real! You're some meat that went bad. Some mustard that didn't agree with me. I'm goin' to bed."

"You were right the first time," Marley said. "You're goin' to hell . . . or anyway, hell's waitin' room. Like me." Marley's voice softened into a plea. "Stoney—help me outa this, pal. Help yourself."

"How?"

"Solve my murder."

Stone blew a smoke ring. "Is that all?"

Marley stood and a howling wind seemed to blow through the apartment, drapes waving like ghosts. *It means something to me!*

Now Stone was sweating; this *was* happening.

"One year ago," Marley said in a deep rumbling voice, "they found me in the alley behind the Bismarck Hotel, my back to the wall, one bullet in the pump, two in the stomach and one in between . . . *remember?*"

And Marley removed the bullet scorched trenchcoat to reveal the four wounds—beams of red neon light from the window behind him cut through Marley like swords through a magician's box.

"Remember?"

Stone was backing up, patting the air with his palms. "Okay, okay . . . why don't you just *tell* me who bumped you off, and I'll settle up for you. Then we'll be square."

"It's not that easy . . . I'm not . . . *allowed* to tell you."

"Who *made* these goddamn rules?"

Marley raised an eyebrow, lifted a finger, pointed up. "Right again. To save us both, you gotta act like a detective . . . you gotta look for clues . . . and you must do this *your-*

23

self . . . though you *will* be aided."

"How?"

"You're gonna have three more visitors."

"Swell! Who's first? Karloff, or Lugosi?"

Marley moved away from the couch, toward the door, shackles clanking. "Don't blow it for the both of us, keed," he said, and left through the door—*through* the door.

Stone stood staring at where his late partner had literally disappeared, and shook his head. Then he went to the bar and poured himself a drink. Soon he was questioning the reality of what had just happened; and, a drink later, he stumbled into his bedroom and flopped onto his bed, fully clothed.

He was sleeping the sound sleep of the dead-drunk when his bed got jostled.

Somebody was kicking it.

Waking to semi-darkness, Stone said, "Who in hell . . ."

Looming over him was a roughly handsome, Clark Gable-mustached figure in a straw hat and a white double-breasted seersucker.

Stone dove for Sadie, his .38 in its shoulder holster slung over his nightstand, but then, in an eyeblink the guy was gone.

"Over here, boyo."

Stone turned and the guy in the jauntily cocked straw hat was standing there, picking his teeth with a toothpick.

"Save yourself the ammo," the guy said. "They already got me."

And he unbuttoned his jacket and displayed several ugly gaping exit wounds.

"In the back," the guy said, "the bastards."

The guy looked oddly familiar. "Who the hell are you?"

"Let's put it this way. If a bunch of trigger-happy feds are chasin' ya, don't duck down that alley by the Biograph—it's a dead-end, brother."

"John Dillinger!"

"Right—only it's a hard 'g,' like in gun: Dillin-*ger*. Okay, sonny? Pet peeve o'mine." Dillinger was buttoning up his jacket.

"You . . . you must not have been killed wearing *that* suit."

"Naw—it's new. Christmas present from the Boss. I got a pretty good racket goin' here—helpin' chumps like you make good. Another five hundred years, and I get sprung."

"How exactly is a cheap crook like you gonna help *me* make good?"

Dillinger grabbed Stone by the shirtfront. Stone took a swing at the ghost, but his hand only passed through.

"There ain't nothin' cheap about John Dillinger! I didn't rob nobody but banks, and times was hard, then, *banks* was the bad guys . . . and I never shot nobody. Otherwise, I'da got the big heat."

"The big heat?"

Dillinger raised an eyebrow and angled a thumb, downward. "Which is where you're headed, sonny, if you don't get your lousy head screwed on right. Come with me."

"Where are we goin'?"

"Into your past. Maybe that's why *I* got picked for this caper—see, I was a Midwest farm kid like you. Come on! Don't make me drag ya . . ."

Reluctantly, Stone followed the spirit into the next room . . .

. . . where Stone found himself not in the living room of his apartment, but in the snowy yard out in front of a small farmhouse. Snowflakes fell lazily upon an idyllic rural winter landscape; an eight-year-old boy was building a snowman.

"I know this place," Stone said.

"You know the *kid,* too," Dillinger said. "It's you. You live in that house."

"Why aren't I cold? It's gotta be freezing, but I feel like I'm still in my apartment."

"You're a shadow here, just like me," Dillinger said.

"Dickie!" a voice called from the porch. "Come inside— you'll catch your death!"

"Ma!" Stone said, and moved toward her. He studied her serene, beautiful face in the doorway. "Ma . . ."

He tried to touch her and his hand passed through.

Behind him, Dillinger said, "I told ya, boyo—you're a shadow. Just lean back and watch . . . maybe you'll learn somethin'."

Then eight-year-old Dickie Stone ran right through the shadow of his future self, and inside the house, closing the door behind him, leaving Stone and Dillinger on the porch.

"Now what?" Stone asked.

"Since when were you shy about breaking and entering?" Dillinger said.

And walked *through* the door . . .

"Look who's talking," Stone said. He took a breath and followed.

Stone found himself in the cozy farmhouse, warmed by a wood-burning stove, which, surprisingly, he could feel. In one corner of the modestly furnished living room stood a pine tree, almost too tall for the room to contain, decorated with tinsel and a star, wrapped gifts scattered under it. A spinet piano hugged a wall. Stone watched his eight-year-old self strip out of an aviator cap and woolen coat and boots and sit at a little table where he began working on a puzzle.

"Five hundred pieces," Stone said. "It's a picture of Tom Mix and his horse what's-his-name."

"Tony," said Dillinger.

"God, will ya smell that pine tree! And my mother's cooking! If I'm a shadow, how come I can smell her cooking?"

"Hey, pal—don't ask me. I'm just the tour guide. Maybe somebody upstairs wants your memory jogged."

Stone moved into the kitchen, where his mother was at the stove, stirring gravy.

"God, that gravy smells good . . . can you smell it?"

"No," said Dillinger.

"She's baking mincemeat pie, too . . . you're *lucky* you can't smell that. Garbage! But Pa always liked it . . ."

"My ma made a mean plum pudding at Christmas," Dillinger said.

"Mine, too! It's bubbling on the stove! Can't you smell it?"

"No! This is *your* past, pal, not mine . . ."

The back door opened and a man in a blue denim coat and woolen knit cap entered, stomping the snow off his work boots.

"That mincemeat pie must be what heaven smells like," the man said. Sky-blue eyes were an incongruously gentle presence in his hard, weathered face.

"Pa," Stone said.

Taking off his jacket, the man walked right through the shadow of his grown son. "Roads are still snowed in," his father told his mother.

"Oh dear! I was so counting on Bob and Helen for Christmas supper!"

"That's my uncle and aunt," Stone told Dillinger. "Bob was Mom's brother."

"They'll be here," Pa Stone said, with a thin smile. "Davey took the horse and buggy into town after them."

"My brother Davey," Stone explained to Dillinger.

"Oh dear," his mother was saying. "He's so frail . . . oh, how could you . . ."

"Send a boy to do a man's job? Sarah, Davey's sixteen. Proud as I am of the boy for his school marks, he's got to learn to be a man. Anyway, he *wanted* to do it. He *likes* to help."

Stone's ma could only say, "Oh dear," again and again.

"Now, Sarah—I'll *not* have these boys babied!"

"Well, the old S.O.B. sure didn't baby *me,*" Stone said to Dillinger.

"Davey just doesn't have Dickie's spirit," said Pa. "Dickie's always getting in scrapes, and he sure don't make the grades Davey does, but the boy's got gumption and guts."

Stone had never known his pa felt that way about him.

"Then why are you so hard on the child, Jess?" his mother was asking. "Last time he got caught playing hookey from school, you gave him the waling of his life."

"How else is the boy to learn? That's how my pa taught *me* the straight and narrow path."

"Straight and narrow razor strap's more like it," Stone said.

Ma was stroking Pa's rough face. "You love both your boys. It's Christmas, Jess. Why don't you tell 'em how you feel?"

"They know," he said gruffly.

Emotions churned in Stone, and he didn't like it. "Tour guide—I've had about all of this I can take . . ."

"Not just yet," Dillinger said. "Let's go in the other room."

They did, but it was suddenly later, after dark, the living room filled with family members sitting on sofas and chairs and even the floor, having cider after a supper that everybody was raving about.

A pudgy, good-natured man in his forties was saying to

eight-year-old Dickie, "How do you like your gift, young man?"

The boy was wearing a policeman's cap and a little tin badge; he also had a miniature nightstick, a pair of handcuffs, and a traffic whistle. "It's the cat's meow, Uncle Bob!"

"Where does he get those vulgar expressions?" his mother asked disapprovingly, but not sternly.

"Cap'n Billy's Whiz Bang," Stone whispered to Dillinger.

"Never missed an issue myself," Dillinger said.

The boy started blowing the whistle shrilly and there was laughter, but the boy's father said, "Enough!"

And the boy obeyed.

The door opened. A boy of sixteen, but skinny and not much taller than Dickie, came in; bundled in winter clothes, he was bringing in a pile of firewood for the wood-burning stove.

"Davey," Stone said.

"Did you like your older brother?" Dillinger asked.

"He was a great guy. You could always depend on him for a smile or a helpin' hand . . . But what did it get him?"

Out of his winter jacket, firewood deposited, Davey went over to his younger brother and ruffled his hair. "Gonna get the bad guys, little brother?"

"I'm gonna bop 'em," Dickie said, "then slap the cuffs on!"

"On Christmas?" Davey asked. "Even crooks got a right to celebrate the Savior's birth, don't ya think?"

"Yeah. Well, okay . . . day *after,* then."

Everybody was laughing as little Dickie swung his nightstick at imaginary felons.

"Dickie my lad," said Uncle Bob, "someday I'll hire you on at the station."

Stone explained to Dillinger: "He was police chief, over at De Kalb."

29

"Peachy," said Dillinger.

Davey said, "Ma—how about sitting down at the piano, and helping put us all in the Yuletide spirit?"

"Yeah, Ma!" said little Dickie. "Tickle the ol' ivories!"

Soon the group was singing carols, Davey leading them: *"God Rest Ye Merry Gentlemen . . ."*

"Seen enough?" Dillinger said.

"Just a second," Stone said. "Let me hear a little more . . . this is the last decent Christmas I can remember. . . ."

After a while, the gaily singing people began to fade, but the room remained, and suddenly Stone saw the figure of his father, kneeling at the window, a rifle in his hands, face contorted savagely. There was no Christmas tree, although Stone knew at once that this was indeed a later Christmas day in his family's history. His mother cowered by the piano; she seemed frightened and on the verge of tears. A fourteen-year-old Dickie was crouched beside his father near the window.

"God," said Stone. "Not *this* Christmas . . ."

"Son," his pa was saying to the teenage Stone, "I want you and your mother to go on out."

"No, Pa! I want to stay beside you! Ma should go, but . . ."

"You're not too big to get your hide tanned, boy."

"Pa . . ."

A voice through a megaphone outside called: "Jess! It's Bob! Let me come in and at least talk!"

"When hell freezes over!" Pa shouted. "Now get off my property, or so help me, I'll shoot you where you stand!"

"Jess, that's my *brother*," Ma said, tears brimming. "And it's . . . it's not *our* property, anymore . . ."

"Whose is it, then? The bank's? Did the bankers work this ground for twenty years? Did the bankers put blood and sweat and years into this land?"

Dillinger elbowed Stone. "*That's* why this country *needed* guys like me. Say—where's your older brother, anyway?"

"Dead," Stone said. "He caught pneumonia the winter of '28 . . . stayed outside for hours and hours, helping get some family's flivver out of a ditch in the wind and cold. All my folks' dreams died with him."

"Let Bob come in," Ma was saying. "Hear him out."

Pa thought it over; he looked so much older, now. Not years older—decades. Finally he said, "All right. For you, Sarah. Just 'cause he's kin of yours."

When the door opened, and Bob came in, he was in full police-chief array, under a fur-lined jacket; the badge on his cap gleamed.

"Jess," he said solemnly, "you're at the end of your string. I wish I could help you, but the bank's foreclosed, and the law's the law."

"Why's the law on *their* side?" teenage Stone asked. "Isn't the law supposed to help everybody equal?"

"People with money get treated a hell of lot more equal, son," his father said bitterly.

"I worked out a deal," Bob said. "You can keep your furniture. I can come over with the paddy wagon and load 'er up with your things; we'll store 'em in my garage. There'll be no charges brought. Helen and I have room for you and Sarah and Dick—you can stay with us till you find something."

The rifle was still in Pa's hands. "*This* is my home, Robert."

"No, Jess—it's a house the bank owns. Your home is your family, and you take them with you. Let me ask you this— what would Davey want you to do?"

Stone looked away; he knew what was coming: one of two times he ever saw his father cry—the other was the night Davey died.

A single tear running down his cheek, Pa said, "How am I supposed to support my family?"

Bob's voice was gentle: "I got friends at the barb-wire factory. Already talked to 'em about you. They'll take you on. Having a job in times like these is a blessing."

Pa nodded. He sighed, handed his rifle over. "Thank you, Robert."

"Yeah, Uncle Bob," teenage Stone said sarcastically. "Merry Christmas! In a rat's ass . . ."

"Richard!" his ma said.

His father slapped him.

"You ever do that to me again, old man," teenage Stone said, pointing a hard finger at his father, "I'll knock your damn block off!"

And as his teenage self rushed out, Stone shook his head. "Jesus! Did I have to say that to him, right then? Poor bastard hits rock bottom, and I find a way to push him down lower. . . ."

Pa was standing rigidly, looking downward, as Ma clung to him in a desperate embrace. Uncle Bob, looking ashamed of himself, trudged out.

"You were just a kid," Dillinger said. "What did you know?"

"Why are you puttin' me through this hell?" Stone demanded. "I can't change the past! What does any of this have to do with finding out who killed Jake Marley?!"

"Don't ask me!" Dillinger flared. "I'm just the damned help!"

The bank robber's ghost stalked out, and Stone—not eager to be left in this part of his past—quickly followed.

Stone now found himself, and his ghostly companion, in the reception area of a small town police station where officers milled and a reception desk loomed. Dillinger led Stone to a partitioned-off office where a Christmas wreath hung on a frosted glass door, which they went through without opening.

Jake Marley, Deputy Chief of Police of De Kalb, Illinois, sat leaned back in his chair, at his desk, smiling as he opened Christmas cards; as he did, cool green cash dropped out of each card.

"Lot of people remembered Jake at Christmas," Stone said.

"Lot of people remember a *lot* of cops at Christmas," Dillinger sneered.

A knock at the door prompted Marley to sweep the cash into a desk drawer. "Yeah?" he called gruffly. "What?"

The uniformed police officer who peaked in was a young Dick Stone. "Deputy Chief Marley? I had word you wanted me to drop by . . . ?"

"Come on in, keed, come on in!" The slick mustached deputy chief gestured magnanimously to the chair opposite his desk. "Take a load off."

Young Stone sat while his future self and the ghost of a public enemy eavesdropped nearby.

Marley's smile tried a little too hard. "Yesterday was your first day on, I understand."

"Yes, sir."

"Well, I just wanted you to know I don't hold it against you, none—you gettin' this job through patronage."

"What's that supposed to mean?"

Marley shrugged. "Nothin'. A guy does what he has to, to get ahead. It's unusual, your Uncle Bob playin' that kinda game, though. He's a real straight arrow."

"Uncle Bob's kind of a square john, but he's family and I stand by him."

"Swell! Admirable, keed. Admirable. But there's things go

on around here that he don't know about . . . and I'd like to keep it that way."

Young Stone frowned. "Such as?"

"Let me put it this way—if you got a fifty-dollar bill every month, for just lookin' the other way . . . if it was for something truly harmless . . . could you sleep at night?"

"Lookin' the other way, how?"

Marley explained that he was from Chicago—in '26, a local congressman greased the wheels for him to land this rural deputy chief slot, so he could do some favors for the Outfit.

"Not so much goin' on now," said Marley, "not like back in dry days, with the Boys had stills out here. Couple roadhouses where people like to have some extra-legal fun . . ."

"Gambling and girls, you mean."

"Right. And there's a farmhouse the Boys use, when things get hot in the city, and a field where they like to do some . . . planting . . . now and then."

"I don't think I could sleep at night, knowing that's going on."

Marley's eyebrows shot up. "Oh?"

"Not for fifty a month." The young officer grinned. "Seventy-five, maybe. A C-note, and I'd be asleep when my head hit the pillow."

Marley stuck his hand across his desk. "I think this is gonna be the start of a beautiful friendship."

They shook hands, but when young Stone brought his hand back, there was a C-note in it.

"Merry Christmas, Mr. Marley."

"Make it 'Jake.' Many happy returns, keed."

Dillinger tugged Stone's arm and they walked through the office wall and were suddenly in another office: the outer office of MARLEY AND STONE: CONFIDENTIAL INVESTIGATIONS. Katie was watering the base of a Christmas tree in the corner.

"This is, what?" Dillinger asked Stone. "Five years ago?"

"Right. Christmas Eve, '37, I think . . ."

Marley was whispering to a five-years younger Stone. "Nice lookin' twist you hired."

"She'll class up the front office. And remember, Jake—I saw her first."

Marley grinned. "What do I need with a kid like her, when I got a woman like Maggie? Ah! Speak of the devil. . . ."

Maggie was entering the outer office on the arm of a blond, boyishly handsome man in a crisp business suit.

"Stoney," Marley said, "meet our biggest client: this is Larry Turner . . . he's the V.P. with Consolidated who's tossing all that investigating our way."

"Couldn't do this without you, Mr. Turner," Stone said.

"Make it 'Larry,' " he said. "Pleasure to do business with such a well-connected firm."

Dillinger said, "What's *this* Boy Scout's angle?"

Stone said, "We been kicking that boy scout back twenty percent of what his firm pays us since day one. I don't know how Jake knew him, but Consolidated was the account that let us leave De Kalb and set up shop in the Loop."

"How'd your Uncle Bob feel about you leaving the force?"

"He damn near cried . . . he always figured I'd step in and fill his shoes someday. Poor yokel . . . just didn't have a clue—all that corruption going on right under his nose."

"By his deputy chief and his nephew, you mean."

Stone said nothing, but the five-year's-ago him was saying to Marley, "Look—this insurance racket is swell. But the real dough is in divorce work."

"You're right, keed. I'm ahead of you . . . we get the incriminating photos of the cheating spouse, then sell 'em to the highest bidder."

"Sweet! That's what they get for not love, honor and obeyin'."

The private eyes shared a big horse laugh. Katie looked their way and smiled, glad to see her bosses enjoying themselves on Christmas Eve.

"Come on," Dillinger said, summoning Stone with a crooked finger.

And the late bank robber walked Stone through a wall into the alley where Jake Marley lay crumpled against a brick wall, between two garbage cans, holes shot in the front of him, eyes wide and empty and staring.

Sgt. Hank Ross was showing the body to Stone. "Thought you better see this, pal. Poor slob never even got his gun out. Still tucked away under his buttoned-up topcoat. Shooter musta been somebody who knew him, don't ya figure?"

Stone shrugged. "You're the homicide dick."

"Now, Stoney . . . I don't want you looking into this. I know he was your partner, and your friend, but . . ."

"You talked me out of it." Stone lighted up a Lucky. "I'll take care of informin' the widow."

Ross just looked at him. Then he said, "Merry goddamn Christmas, Stoney."

"In a rat's ass," he said, turning away from his dead partner.

"Jeez!" Dillinger said. "That's cold! Couldn't ya squeeze out just one tear for your old pal?"

Stone said nothing. His year-ago self walked right through him.

"You want the truth, Dillin-*ger*? All I was thinkin' was, with all the people he jacked around, Jake was lucky to've lived *this* long. And how our partnership agreement spelled out that the business was mine, now."

"Hell! I thought *Gillis* was cold."

"Gillis?"

"Lester Gillis. Baby Face Nelson to you. Come on, sonny. You and me reached the end of the line."

And Dillinger shoved Stone, hard—right through the brick wall; and when the detective blinked again, he was alone on his bed, in his apartment.

He sat up; rubbed his eyes, scratched his head. "Meat shortage or not, that salami gets pitched. . . ."

He flopped back on the bed, still fully dressed, and stared at the ceiling; the dream was hanging with him—thoughts, images, of his mother, father, brother, even Marley, floated in front of him, speaking to him . . .

Out in the other room, the doorbell rang, startling him. He checked the round Bakelite clock on his nightstand: two a.m. Who in hell would be calling on him at this hour?

On the other hand, he thought as he stumbled out to his door, *talking to somebody with a pulse would be nice for a change . . .*

And there on his doorstep was a crisply uniformed soldier, a freshly scrubbed young man with his overseas cap tugged down onto his forehead.

"Mr. Stone?"

"Ben? Is that *you?* Ben Crockett!" Stone's grin split his face. "Katie's little brother, back from the wars—is *she* gonna be tickled!"

The boy seemed somewhat dazed as he stepped inside.

"Uh, Ben . . . if you're lookin' for Katie, she's at her place tonight."

"I'm here to see *you,* Mr. Stone."

"Well, that's swell, kid . . . but why?"

"I'm not really sure," the boy said. "May I sit down?"

"Sure, kid, sure! You want something to drink?"

"No thanks. You'll have to excuse me, sir—I'm kinda confused. The briefing I got . . . it was pretty screwy."

"Briefing?"

"Yeah. This is a temporary assignment. But they said I was 'uniquely qualified' for this mission."

"What do they want you to do, kid? Haul me down for another physical?"

"That reminds me!" Private Crockett dug into a pocket and found a scrap of paper. "Does this mean anything to you? 'Tell the 4-F Mr. Stone he really *does* have flat feet and the doctor he paid off was scamming *him*.' "

Stone's mouth dropped open, then he laughed. "Well, that's a Chicago doc for ya. So, is that the extent of your 'mission'?"

The boy tucked the scrap of paper away. "No. There's more . . . and it's *weird*. I'm supposed to tell you to go look in the mirror."

"Look in the mirror?"

"Yeah—that one over there, I guess."

"Kid . . ."

"Please, Mr. Stone. I don't think I get to go home for Christmas till I get this done."

Stone sighed, said okay, and shuffled over to the mirror near his console radio; he saw his now unshaven, slightly bleary-eyed reflection, and the boy in his trim overseas cap looking gravely over his shoulder. "Now what, kid?"

"You're supposed to look in there, is all. I was told you're gonna see tomorrow . . . or, actually, it's after midnight already, ain't it? Anyway, Christmas day, 1942 . . ."

And the mirror before Stone became a window.

Through the window, he saw Maggie Marley and Larry Turner, the insurance company V.P., toasting cocktail glasses—Maggie in a negligee, Turner in a silk smoking jacket; they were snuggled on a couch in her fancy apartment.

"What the hell's this?" Stone asked. "Maggie and that snake Turner . . . since when are *they* an item?"

"How much longer," Maggie was saying to Turner, "do I have to put up with him?"

"You *need* Stone," Turner said, nuzzling her neck. "He's your alibi, baby."

"But I didn't *kill* Jake!"

"Sure you didn't. Sure you didn't. . . . Anyway, string him along a little way, then let him down easy. . . . Right now you still need him in your pocket. He helped you get Eddie off your tail, didn't he?"

Maggie frowned. "Well . . . you're right about that. But his touch . . . it makes my skin crawl . . ."

"Why you little . . ." Stone began.

But the images on the mirror blurred, and were replaced with another image: Eddie Marley, in his sleazy little apartment, not answering his door, cowering as somebody out there was banging with a fist.

"Let us in, Eddie! We got a Christmas present for ya!"

Eddie, sweating, shaking like crazy, looked at a framed photo of his late brother Jake.

"How could you do this to me, Jake?" he whispered. "You promised you'd take care of me . . ."

The door splintered open and two Outfit thugs—huge hulking faceless creatures in topcoats and fedoras—cornered him quickly.

"Gimme another week, fellas! I can get ya five C's today, to tide us over till then!"

"Too late, Eddie," one ominous goon said. "You kept the Outfit waitin' just one time too many. . . ."

A hand filled itself with a .45 automatic that erupted once, twice, three times. Eddie crumpled to the floor, bleeding. Dying.

"Jake . . . Jake . . . you let me down . . . you promised. . . ."

The mirror blurred again. Stone looked at Private Crockett. "Is that a done deal, kid? If that's gonna happen Christmas day, can't I still bail that little weasel out . . . ?"

"I don't know, Mr. Stone. They didn't tell me that."

A new image began to form on the mirror: Stone's young employee, Joey Ernest, seated in his living room, by a fireplace, looking glum—in fact, he seemed on the verge of tears. Nearby, his little boy of six and his little girl of four were playing with some nice new toys under a tree bright with Christmas lights.

Joey's wife Linda, a pretty blonde in a red Christmas dress, came over and slipped an arm around him.

"Why are you so blue, darling?"

"I can't help it. . . . I know I should be happy. It's been a great Christmas . . . but I feel so . . . so ashamed. . . ."

"Darling . . ."

"Other guys my age, they're fighting on bloody beaches to preserve the honor and glory of God and country. Me, I crawl around under beds and hide in hotel closets and take dirty pictures of adulterers."

"Joey! The children!"

"I know! The children. . . . I want to give them a good life . . . but do I have to do it like this? Covering up for my philandering boss, among a million other indignities? I'm quitting! I'm swear, I'm quitting Monday!"

She kissed his cheek. "Then I'll stand right beside you."

He gave her a hangdog look. "I shouldn't have got us so far in over our heads with all these time payments. . . . How are we gonna make it, Linda?"

"I'm going to take that job at the defense plant. Mom can

look after the kids, when one of us isn't here. It's going to be fine."

"Aw, Linda. I love you so much. Merry Christmas, baby."

"Merry Christmas, darling."

They were embracing as the image blurred.

Now the mirror filled with a tableau of homeless men in a soup kitchen. They were standing in line, receiving soup and bread and a hot meal. Serving them was the pretty young Salvation Army worker Stone made a pass at, at the office. In the background, voices of men at the mission were singing a carol: *"God Rest Ye Merry Gentlemen."*

"We used to sing that song at home," Stone told the soldier. "My ma would play the piano. Christ! What a heel."

"Who, Mr. Stone?"

But the image on the mirror was different again: Katie Crockett and a plump older woman and a frail-looking older man . . .

"Hey, kid," Stone said, "it's your sister!"

"And my folks," he said quietly.

. . . sitting around the Christmas tree in Katie's little apartment, opening presents and chatting happily. The doorbell rang, and Katie bounced up to answer it.

But she didn't come bouncing back.

"It's . . . it's a telegram from the war department," Katie said.

"Oh no!" her mother said. "Not . . ."

"It's Ben, isn't it?" her father said.

They huddled together and read the telegram and tears streamed down their faces.

"Well, that's wrong, kid," Stone said to Private Crockett. "You gotta go there tomorrow, and straighten that out. It's breaking their hearts—they think you're dead!"

"Mr. Stone," the boy said, removing his overseas cap, revealing the bullet hole in the center of his forehead, "I'm afraid they're right."

"God . . ."

"I have to go home now," he said. "Tell sis I love her, would you, Mr. Stone? And the folks, too?"

The young soldier, like another image blurring in the mirror, faded away.

Alone in his bedroom again, Stone held his throbbing head in his hands. "Did somebody slip me a mickey or something?" Exhausted, he stumbled back to his bed, falling face first, and sleep, mercifully, descended.

I'll have a blue Christmas . . .

Stone's eyes popped open; his bedroom was still dark. Someone was singing, a sort of hillbilly Bing Crosby, a strange voice, an earthy unearthly voice. . . .

. . . blue Christmas, that's certain . . .

The little round clock said 4 a.m.

. . . decorations of white . . .

"What the hell is that racket? The radio?"

"It's me, sir," the same voice said. Mellow, baritone, slurry.

Stone hauled himself off the bed and beheld the strangest apparition of all: the man standing before him wore a white leather outfit with a cape, glittering with rhinestones. The (slightly overweight) man had longish jet-black hair, an insolently handsome if puffy face, and heavy-lidded eyes.

"Who the hell are you?"

"Ah don't mean to soun' immodest, sir," he said huskily, "but where ah come from they call me 'the King.'"

"Don't tell me *you're* Jesus Christ!" Stone said, eyes popping.

"Not hardly, sir. Ah'm just a poor country boy. Right now, ah'd be about seven years old, sir."

"If you're seven years old, I'd cut down on the Baby Ruths, if I was you."

The apparition in white moved toward him, a leather ghost; his shoes were strange, too—rhinestone-studded white cowboy boots. "Ah'm afraid you don't understand, sir—ah'm the ghost of somebody who hasn't growed up and lived yet, in your day . . . let alone died."

"You haven't died yet, but you're a ghost? A ghost in a white-leather zoot suit! This is the best one yet. This is my favorite so far . . ."

"See, ah was a very famous person, or ah'm goin' to be. Ah really don't mean to brag, but ah was bigger than the Beatles."

"You're the biggest bug I ever saw, period, pal."

"Sir, ah abused my talent, and my body, so ah'm payin' some dues. That's how come ah got this gig."

" 'Gig'?"

"Ah'm here to show you a little preview of comin' attractions, sir. Somethin' that's gonna go down 'long about next Christmas . . . Christmas of '43. . . ."

The apparition struck a strange pose, as if turning his entire body into a pointing arrow, and suddenly both the King and Stone were in a small chapel, bedecked rather garishly with Christmas decorations that seemed un-churchlike, somehow.

"Where *are* we?"

"Welcome to *my* world, sir. We're a few years early to appreciate it, but someday, this is gonna be a real bright light city."

"What are you *talkin'* about?"

The King grinned sideways. "We're in Vegas, man!"

Up at the front of the chapel, a man and woman faced a minister. Canned organ music was filtering in. A wedding ceremony was under way.

Stone walked up to have a look.

"I'll be damned," Stone said.

"That's what we're tryin' to prevent, sir."

"It's Maggie and that creep Larry Turner! Getting hitched! Well, good riddance to both of 'em. . . ."

"Maybe you oughta see how *you're* spendin' next Christmas. . . ."

And now Stone and the rhinestone ghost were in a jail cell. So was a haggard looking, next year's Stone—in white-and-black prison garb, seated on his cot, looking desperate. On a stool across from him was Sgt. Hank Ross.

"Hank, you *know* I'm innocent!"

"I believe you, Stoney. But the jury didn't. That eye witness held up . . ."

"He was bought and paid for!"

". . . and your gun turning out to be the murder weapon, well. . . ."

"You get an anonymous phone tip to match the slugs that killed Jake with my gun, a *year* later, and you don't think that's suspicious?"

"The ballistics tests were positive."

"Some crooked cop must've switched the real bullets with some phonies shot from my gun! I told you, Hank, when I went to Miami on vacation, I left the gun in my desk drawer. Anybody coulda . . ."

"Old news, Stoney."

"You gotta believe me!"

"I do. But with your appeal turned down. . . ."

"What about the governor?"

"The papers want your ass, and the governor wants votes. You know how it works."

"Yeah, Hank. I know how it works, all right. . . ."

"Stoney, better put things right between you and your maker." Ross sighed, heavily. " 'Cause tomorrow about now . . . you're gonna be meetin' him."

Ross patted his friend on the shoulder, called for the guard and was soon gone. Stone stood and clung onto the bars of his cell as a forlorn harmonica played "Come All Ye Faithful."

"Death row?" Stone said to the King. "Next Christmas, I'm on death row?"

"Sir, ah'm afraid that's right. And ah think we're gonna have to be movin' on. . . ."

And they were back in the apartment.

"I have no idea who the hell you are," Stone said, "but I owe you. Of all the visions I've seen tonight, yours are the ones that brought it all home to me."

"Thank you vurry much," the King said.

Stone glanced away, but when he turned back, his visitor had left the building.

Almost dizzy, Stone fell back onto bed, head whirling; sleep descended. . . .

When he awakened, it was almost noon. He felt re-born. He showered and shaved, whistling "Joy to the World." As he got dressed, he slung on his shoulder-holstered revolver, removing the gun and checking its cylinder.

"Jeez, Sadie," Stone said. "What kinda girl *are* you? Loaded on Christmas. . . ."

Chuckling, he tucked the gun in its holster, then frowned and had a closer look at the .38, studying its handle.

"I'll be damned," he said to himself. Then he smiled knowingly. ". . . Or maybe not."

He slipped the gun back in its hand-tooled shoulder holster, tossed on his topcoat. Then, as an afterthought, he went to his wall safe and counted out $5,000 in C notes, and folded the wad in his pocket.

When Stone knocked at Eddie's apartment, there was no answer. Was he too late? He yelled: "Eddie—it's Stone! I got your cash. All five grand of it!"

Finally Eddie peeked out; he was a little bruised up from the rough handling Stone gave him last night. "What is this—a gag?"

"No. Lemme in."

In the little apartment—strewn with old issues of *Racing News,* dirty clothes and take-out dinner cartons—Stone counted the cash out to a stunned Eddie.

"What is this?"

"It's a Christmas present, you little weasel."

"Why . . . ?"

"You're my partner's brother. I had a responsibility to help you out. But this is *it* . . . this'll bail you out today, and don't ask me for no more bail-outs in the future, got it? When the goons come, pay 'em off. And if you wanna lose your gambling habit, I might find some legwork for you to do, at the office. But otherwise, you're on your own."

"I don't get it. Why help me, after I tried to blackmail you. . . ."

"Oh, well, I'll break your arms if you try *that* again."

"Now, that sounds like the old Stoney."

"No—the old Stoney woulda killed you. Eddie—you said your brother promised to 'take care of' you, if anything happened to him. You seemed real sure of that."

Eddie nodded emphatically. "He told me I was on his insurance policy—fifty percent was supposed to go to me, but somehow that witch wound up with *all* of it!"

Before long, Stone was knocking at the penthouse apartment door of the widow Marley. Maggie tried not to betray her discomfort at seeing Stone. "Why, Richard," she said, raising her voice, "what a lovely Christmas surpri . . ."

But he pushed past her, before Larry Turner could find a hiding place. Turner was caught by the fireplace, where no stockings were hung.

"Merry Christmas, Larry," Stone said. "I got a present for ya. . . ."

Stone pulled the .38 out from under his shoulder and pointed it at the trembling Turner, who wore the silk smoking jacket Stone had seen in the vision in the mirror last night.

"Actually, it's a present *you* gave *me,*" Stone said. "My best friend—my best girl—is Sadie. My gun. Kind of a sad commentary, ain't it?"

"I don't know what's gotten into you, Stone. . . . Just don't point that thing at me . . ."

"Funny thing is, this isn't Sadie. Imagine—me goin' around with the wrong dame for over a year, and not knowin' it!"

Maggie said, "Richard, please put that gun away—"

"Sweetheart, would you mind standin' over there by your boyfriend? I honestly don't think you were in on this, but I'm not takin' any chances."

She started to say something, and Stone said, "Move!" and, with the .38, waved her over by Turner.

Stone continued: "Sometime last year, Larry . . . I don't know when exactly, just that it had to be before Christmas Eve . . . you stole my Sadie, and substituted a similar gun. Trouble is, Sadie has a little chip out of the handle . . . tiny, but it's there, only it's *not* there on *this* gun."

"Why in hell would I do that?" Turner asked.

"Because you wanted to use *my* gun to kill Jake with. Which you did."

"Kill Jake! Why would I . . ."

"Because you and Maggie are an item. A secret item, but an item. You fixed her insurance policy so that *all* those

47

double-indemnity dollars went to her, even though Jake intended his no-good brother get half. Jake considered you a friend—that's why his hands were in his pockets, and his gun under his coat, when you got up close to him and sent him those thirty-eight caliber Christmas greetings."

"With *your* gun? If any of this were true, I'd have given that gun to the police, long ago."

"Not necessarily. You're an insurance man . . . using my gun was like takin' out a policy. Any time it looked like suspicion was headed your way, or even Maggie's, you could switch guns again and make a nice little anonymous call."

Maggie was watching Turner, eyes wide, horror growing. "Is this true? Did you kill Jake?"

"It's nonsense," Turner told her dismissively.

"Well, then," she said bitterly, "what was that gun you had me put in my wall safe? For my 'protection,' you said!"

"Shut-up," he said.

"Now I know what *I* want for Christmas," Stone said. "Maggie, open the safe."

She went to an oil painting of herself, removed it, and revealed the round safe, which she opened.

"Stand aside, sweetheart," Stone said, "and let *him* get the gun out."

Turner, sweating, licked his lips and reached in and grabbed the gun, wheeled, fired, dove behind the nearby couch. When Turner peeked around to fire again at Stone, the detective had already dropped to the floor. Stone returned fire, his slug piercing a plump couch cushion. Turner popped up again, and Stone nailed him through the shoulder.

Turner yelped and fell, his dropped gun spinning away harmlessly on the marble floor.

Stone stood over Turner, who looked up in anger and anguish, holding onto his shot-up shoulder. "You *wanted* me to try to shoot it out with you!"

"That's right."

"*Why?*"

" 'Cause it was all theory till you tried to shoot me. Now it'll hold up with the cops and in court."

"You bastard, Stone . . . why don't you just do it? Why don't just shoot me and be the hell done with it?"

"I don't think so. First of all, I like the idea of you spendin' next Christmas on death row. Second, you're not worth goin' to hell over."

Stone phoned Sgt. Ross. "Yeah, I know you're at home, Hank—but I got another present for ya—all gift-wrapped. . . ."

He hung up, then found himself facing a slyly smiling Maggie.

"No hard feelings?" she asked.

"Naw. We were both louses. Both running around on each other."

Maggie was looking at him seductively; running a finger up and down his arm. "You were so *sexy* shooting it out like that. . . . I don't think I was ever more attracted to you. . . ."

He just laughed, shook his head, pushed her gently aside.

"I would rather go to hell," he said.

Later, with Turner turned over to Ross, Stone stopped at Joey Ernest's house out in the north suburbs.

"Mr. Stone—what are you . . . ?"

"I just wanted to wish you a Merry Christmas, kid. And tell you my New Year's resolution is to dump the divorce racket."

"Really?"

"Really. There's some retail credit action we can get. . . . It won't pay the big bucks, but we'll be able to look at ourselves in the mirror."

Joey's face lighted up. "You don't know what this means to me, Mr. Stone!"

"I think maybe I do. Incidentally, Mrs. Marley and me are kaput. No more covering up for your dirty boss."

"Mr. Stone . . . come in and say hello to the family. We haven't sat down to dinner yet. Please join us!"

"I'd love to say hi, but I can't stay long. I have another engagement."

Finally, he knocked at the door of Katie's little apartment.

"Why . . . Richard!" Her beaming face told him that certain news hadn't yet reached her.

"Can a guy change his mind? And his ways? I'd love to have Christmas with you and your folks."

She slipped her arm in his and ushered him in. "Oh, they'll be so thrilled to meet you! You've made me so happy, Richard. . . ."

"I just wanted to be with you today," he said, "and maybe sometime, before New Year's, we could drive over to De Kalb and see my Uncle Bob and Aunt Helen."

"That would be lovely!" she said, as she walked him into the living room with its sparkling Christmas tree. Her mother and father rose from the couch with smiles.

It would be a blue Christmas for this family, when the doorbell rang, as it would all too soon; but when it did, Stone at least wanted to be with them.

With Katie.

And when they would eventually go to the young soldier's grave, to say a prayer and lay a wreath, Stone would do the same for his late friend and partner.

MOTHER'S DAY

Mommy

The mother and daughter in the hallway of John F. Kennedy Grade School were each other's picture-perfect reflection.

Mommy wore a tailored pink suit with high heels, her blonde hair short and perfectly coifed; pearls caressed the shapely little woman's pale throat, and a big black purse was tucked under her arm. Daughter, in a frilly white blouse with a pink skirt and matching tights, was petite, too, a head smaller than her mother. Their faces were almost identical—heart-shaped, with luminous china-blue eyes, long lashes, cupid's bow mouths, and creamy complexions.

The only difference between them was Mommy's serene, Madonna-like countenance; the little girl was frowning. The frown was not one of disobedience—Jessica Ann Sterling was as well-behaved a modern child as you might hope to find—but a frown of frustration.

"Please don't, Mommy," she said. "I don't want you to make Mrs. Withers mad at me. . . ."

"It's only a matter of what's fair," Mommy said. "You have better grades than that little foreign student."

"He's not foreign, Mommy. Eduardo is Hispanic, and he's a good student, too. . . ."

"Not as good as you." Mommy's smile was a beautiful thing; it could warm up a room. "The award is for 'Out-

51

standing Student of the Year.' You have straight A's, perfect attendance, you're the best student in the 'Talented and Gifted' group."

"Yes, Mommy, but . . ."

"No 'buts,' dear. *You* deserve the 'Outstanding Student' award. Not this little Mexican."

"But Mommy, it's just a stupid plaque. I don't need another. I got one last year . . ."

"And the year before, and the year before that—and you deserve it again this year. Perhaps it's best you go out and wait in the car for Mommy." She looked toward the closed door of the fifth-grade classroom. "Perhaps this should be a private conference. . . ."

"Mommy, please don't embarrass me!"

"I would never do that. Now. Who's your best friend?"

"You are, Mommy."

"Who loves you more than anything on God's green earth?"

"You do, Mommy."

The little girl, head lowered, shuffled down the hall.

"Jessica Ann . . ."

She turned, hope springing. "Yes, Mommy?"

Mommy shook her finger in the air, gently. "Posture."

"Yes, Mommy . . ."

And the little girl went out to wait in their car.

Thelma Withers enjoyed decorating her classroom. She did it as much for herself as the children; not only was it a creative outlet, but the sterile concrete-block classroom could always use some livening up.

Now, with Easter around the corner, she was happy to have the excuse of the upcoming Spring Fling to drape her classroom with pink and yellow crepe paper, and staple her bulletin boards with colorful construction-paper tulips, birds and balloons.

She was proudest of her bulletin board headed "A Spring Bouquet," with a construction-paper bouquet's blossoms consisting of pasted pictures of the faces of children of various ethnic groups, clipped from magazines, smiling in a human array of colors and cultures.

The tall, big-boned teacher was on a stepladder stapling above the green chalkboard a computer print-out banner with the words KENNEDY SCHOOL SPRING FLING bracketed by flowers, when Mrs. Sterling's knock at the open door startled her.

Looking over her shoulder, grappling with the long, somewhat awkward-to-handle banner, Thelma Withers said, "Good afternoon, Mrs. Sterling. I hope you don't mind if I continue with my decorating . . ."

"We did have an appointment for a conference."

What a pain this woman was. The child, Jessica Ann, was a wonderful little girl, and a perfect student, but the mother—what a monster! In almost thirty years of teaching, Thelma had never had one like her—constantly pestering her about imagined slights to her precious child.

"Mrs. Sterling, we had our conference for the quarter just last week. I really want to have these decorations up for the children, and if you don't mind, we'll just talk while . . ."

"I don't mind," the woman said coldly. She was standing at the desk, staring at the shining gold wall plaque for "Outstanding Student of the Year" that was resting there. Her face was expressionless, yet there was something about the woman's eyes that told Thelma Withers just how covetous of the award she was.

Shaking her head, Mrs. Withers turned back to her work, stapling the banner in place.

53

The click clack of the woman's high heels punctuated the sound of stapling as Mrs. Sterling approached.

"You're presenting that plaque tonight, at the PTA meeting," she said.

"That's right," Mrs. Withers said, her back still to the woman.

"You *know* that my daughter deserves that award."

"Your daughter is a wonderful student, but so is Eduardo Melindez."

"Are his grades as good as Jessica Ann's?"

Mrs. Withers stopped stapling and glanced back at the woman, literally looking down her nose at Jessica Ann's mother.

"Actually, Mrs. Sterling, that's none of your business. How I arrive at who the 'Outstanding Student' is is my affair."

"Really."

"Really. Eduardo faces certain obstacles your daughter does not. When someone like Eduardo excels, it's important to give him recognition."

"Because he's a Mexican, you're taking the award away from my daughter? You're punishing her for being white, and for coming from a nice family?"

"That's not how I look at it. A person of color like Eduardo . . ."

"You're not going to give the award to Jessica, are you?"

"It's been decided."

"There's no name engraved on the plaque. It's not too late."

With a disgusted sigh, Mrs. Withers turned and glared at the woman. "It is too late. What are you teaching your daughter with this behavior, Mrs. Sterling?"

"What are you teaching her, when you take what's rightfully hers and give it to somebody because he's a 'person of color'?"

"I don't have anything else to say to you, Mrs. Sterling. Good afternoon." And Mrs. Withers turned back to her stapling, wishing she were stapling this awful woman's head to the wall.

It was at that moment that the ladder moved, suddenly, and the teacher felt herself losing balance, and falling, and she tumbled through the air and landed on her side, hard, the wind knocked out of her.

Moaning, Mrs. Withers opened her eyes, trying to push herself up. Her eyes were filled with the sight of Mrs. Sterling leaning over her, to help her up.

She thought.

Jessica Ann watched as one of the JFK front doors opened and Mommy walked from the building to the BMW, her big purse snugged tightly to her. Mommy wore a very serious expression, almost a frown.

Mommy opened the car door and leaned in.

"Is something wrong?" Jessica Ann asked.

"Yes," she said. "There's been a terrible accident . . . when I went to speak to Mrs. Withers, she was lying on the floor."

"On the floor?"

"She'd been up a ladder, decorating the room for you children. She must have been a very thoughtful teacher."

"Mommy—you make it sound like . . ."

"She's dead, dear. I think she may have broken her neck."

"Mommy . . ." Tears began to well up. Jessica Ann thought the world of Mrs. Withers.

"I stopped at the office and had the secretary phone for an

ambulance. I think we should stay around until help comes, don't you?"

"Yes, Mommy. . . ."

An ambulance came, very soon, its siren screaming, but for no reason: when Mrs. Withers was wheeled out on a stretcher, she was all covered up. Jessica bit her finger and watched and tried not to cry. Mommy stood beside her, patting her shoulder.

"People die, dear," Mommy said. "It's a natural thing."

"What's natural about falling off a ladder, Mommy?"

"Is that a smarty tone?"

"No, Mommy."

"I don't think Mrs. Withers would want you speaking to your mother in a smarty tone."

"No, Mommy."

"Anyway, people fall off ladders all the time. You know, more accidents occur at home than anywhere else."

"Mrs. Withers wasn't at home."

"The work place is the next most frequent."

"Can we go now?"

"No. I'll need to speak to these gentlemen. . . ."

A police car was pulling up; they hadn't bothered with a siren. Maybe somebody called ahead to tell them Mrs. Withers was dead.

Two uniformed policemen questioned Mommy, and then another policeman, in a wrinkled suit and loose tie, talked to Mommy, too. Jessica Ann didn't see him arrive; they were all sitting at tables in the school library, now. Jessica Ann was seated by herself, away from them, but she could hear some of the conversation.

The man in the suit and tie was old—probably forty—and he didn't have much hair on the top of his head, though he did have a mustache. He was kind of pudgy and seemed grouchy.

He said to Mommy, "You didn't speak to Mrs. Withers at all?"

"How could I? She was on the floor with her neck broken."

"You had an appointment . . ."

"Yes. A parent/teacher conference. Anything else, Lt. March?"

"No. Not right now, ma'am."

"Thank you," Mommy said. She stood. "You have my address, and my number. . . ."

"Yeah," he said. "I got your number."

He was giving Mommy a mean look but she just smiled as she gathered her purse and left.

Soon they were driving home. Mommy was humming a song, but Jessica Ann didn't recognize it. One of those old songs, from the '80s.

It was funny—her mother didn't seem very upset about Mrs. Withers' accident at all.

But sometimes Mommy was that way about things.

Jessica Ann loved their house on Rockwell Road. It had been built a long time ago—1957, Mommy said—but it was really cool: light brick and dark wood and a lot of neat angles—a split-level ranch style was how she'd heard her Mommy describe it. They had lived here for two years, ever since Mommy married Mr. Sterling.

Mr. Sterling had been really old—fifty-one, it said in the paper when he died—but Mommy loved him a lot. He had an insurance agency, and was kind of rich—or so they had thought.

She had overheard her Mommy talking to Aunt Beth about it. Aunt Beth was a little older than mommy, and she was pretty too, but she had dark hair. They reminded Jessica Ann of Betty and Veronica in the Archie comic books.

Anyway, one time Jessica Ann heard Mommy in an odd voice, almost a mean voice, complaining that Mr. Sterling hadn't been as rich as he pretended to be. Plus, a lot of his money and property and stuff wound up with his children by (and Mommy didn't usually talk this way, certainly not in front of Jessica Ann) "the first two bitches he was married to."

Still, they had wound up with this cool house.

Jessica Ann missed Mr. Sterling. He was a nice man, before he had his heart attack and died. The only thing was, she didn't like having to call him "Daddy." Her real daddy—who died in the boating accident when she was six—was the only one who deserved being called that.

She kept Daddy's picture by her bed and talked to him every night. She remembered him real good—he was a big, handsome man with shoulders so wide you couldn't look at them both at the same time. He was old, too—even older than Mr. Sterling—and had left them "well off" (as Mommy put it).

Jessica Ann didn't know what had happened to Daddy's money—a few times Mommy talked about "bad investments"—but fortunately Mr. Sterling had come along about the time Daddy's money ran out.

When Jessica Ann and her mother got home from the school, Aunt Beth—who lived a few blocks from them, alone, because she was divorced from Uncle Bob—was waiting dinner. Mommy had called her from JFK and asked if she'd help.

As Jessica Ann came in, Aunt Beth was all over her, bending down, putting her arm around her. It made Jessica Ann uneasy. She wasn't used to displays of affection like that—Mommy talked about loving her a lot, but mostly kept her distance.

"You poor dear," Aunt Beth said. "Poor dear." She looked up at Mommy, who was hanging up both their coats in the closet. "Did she see . . . ?"

"No," Mommy said, shutting the closet door. "I discovered the body. Jessica Ann was in the car."

"Thank God!" Aunt Beth said. "Do either of you even feel like eating?"

"I don't know," Jessica Ann said.

"Sure," Mommy said. "Smells like spaghetti."

"That's what it is," Aunt Beth said. "I made a big bowl of salad, too. . . ."

"I think I'll go to my room," Jessica Ann said.

"No!" Mommy said. "A little unpleasantness isn't going to stand in the way of proper nutrition."

Aunt Beth was frowning, but it was a sad frown. "Please . . . if she doesn't want . . ."

Mommy gave Aunt Beth the "mind your own business" look. Then she turned to Jessica Ann, and pointed to the kitchen. "Now, march in there, young lady. . . ."

"Yes, Mommy."

"Your salad, too."

"Yes, Mommy."

After dinner, Jessica Ann went to her room, a pink world of stuffed animals and Barbie dolls; she had a frilly four-poster bed that Mommy got in an antique shop. She flopped onto it and thought about Mrs. Withers. Thought about what a nice lady Mrs. Withers was. . . .

She was crying into her pillow when Aunt Beth came in.

"There, there," Aunt Beth said, sitting on the edge of the bed, patting the girl's back. "Get it out of your system."

"Do . . . do you think Mrs. Withers had any children?"

"Probably. Maybe even grandchildren."

"Do you . . . do you think I should write them a letter, about what a good teacher she was?"

Aunt Beth's eyes filled up with tears and she clutched Jessica Ann to her. This time Jessica Ann didn't mind. She clutched back, crying into her aunt's blouse.

"I think that's a wonderful idea."

"I'll write it tonight, and add their names later, when I find them out."

"Fine. Jessy . . ." Aunt Beth was the only grown-up who ever called her that; Mommy didn't like nicknames. ". . . you know, your mother . . . she's kind of a . . . special person."

"What do you mean?"

"Well . . . it's just that . . . she has some wonderful qualities."

"She's very smart. And pretty."

"Yes."

"She does everything for me."

"She does a lot for you. But . . . she doesn't always *feel* things like she should."

"What do you mean, Aunt Beth?"

"It's hard to explain. She was babied a lot . . . there were four of us, you know, and she was the youngest. Your grandparents, rest their souls, gave her everything. And why not? She was so pretty, so perfect. . . ."

"She always got her way, didn't she?"

"How did you know that, Jessica Ann?"

"I just do. 'Cause she still does, I guess."

"Jessy . . . I always kind of looked after your mother . . . protected her."

"What do you mean?"

"Just . . . as you grow older, try to understand . . . try to forgive her when she seems . . . if she seems . . ."

"Cold?"

Aunt Beth nodded. Smiled sadly. "Cold," she said. "In her way, she loves you very much."

"I know."

"I have dessert downstairs. You too blue for chocolate cake?"

"Is Mark here? I thought I heard his car."

"He's here," Aunt Beth said, smiling. "And he's asking for you. Mark and chocolate cake—that's quite a combo. . . ."

Jessica Ann grinned, took a tissue from the box on her nightstand, dried her eyes, took her aunt's hand, and allowed herself to be led from her room down the half-stairs.

Mommy's new boyfriend, Mark Jeffries, was in the living room sitting in Mr. Sterling's recliner, sipping an iced tea.

"There's my girl!" he said, as Jessica Ann came into the room; Aunt Beth was in the kitchen with Mommy.

Mark sat forward in the chair, then stood—he was younger than either Mr. Sterling or Daddy, and really good looking, like a soap opera actor with his sandy hair and gray sideburns and deep tan. He wore a green sweater and new jeans and a big white smile. Also, a Rolex watch.

She went quickly to him, and he bent down and hugged her. He smelled good—like lime.

He pushed her gently away and looked at her with concern in his blue-gray eyes. "Are you okay, angel?"

"Sure."

"Your mommy told me about today. Awful rough." He took her by the hand and led her to the couch. He sat down and nodded for her to join him. She did.

"Angel, if you need somebody to talk to . . ."

"I'm fine, Mark. Really."

61

"You know . . . when I was ten, my Boy Scout leader died. He was killed in an automobile accident. I didn't have a dad around . . . he and mom were divorced . . . and my Scout leader was kind of a . . . surrogate father to me. You know what that is?"

"Sure. He kind of took the place of a dad."

"Right. Anyway, when he died, I felt . . . empty. Then I started to get afraid."

"Afraid, Mark?"

"I started to think about dying for the first time. I had trouble. I had nightmares. For the first time I realized nobody lives forever. . . ."

Jessica Ann had known that for a long time. First Daddy, then Mr. Sterling. . . .

"I hope you don't have trouble like that," he said. "But if you do—I just want you to know . . . I'm here for you."

She didn't say anything—just beamed at him.

She was crazy about Mark. Jessica Ann hoped he and Mommy would get married. She thought she could even feel comfortable calling him "Daddy." Maybe.

Mommy had met Mark at a country club dance last month. He had his own business—some kind of mail-order thing that was making a lot of money, she heard Mommy say—and had moved to Ferndale to get away from the "urban blight" where he used to live.

Jessica Ann found she could talk to Mark better than any grown-up she'd ever met. Even better than Aunt Beth. And as much as Jessica Ann loved her Mommy, they didn't really *talk*—no shared secrets, or problems.

But Mark put Jessica Ann at ease. She could talk to him about problems at school or even at home.

"Who wants dessert?" Aunt Beth called.

Soon Jessica Ann and Mark were sitting at the kitchen

table while Mommy, in her perfect white apron (she never got anything on it, so why did she wear it?), was serving up big pieces of chocolate cake.

"I'll just have the ice cream," Aunt Beth told Mommy.

"What's *wrong* with me?" Mommy said. "You're allergic to chocolate! How thoughtless of me."

"Don't be silly . . ."

"How about some strawberry compote on that ice cream?"

"That does sound good."

"There's a jar in the fridge," Mommy said.

Aunt Beth found the jar, but was having trouble opening it.

"Let me have a crack at that," Mark said, and took it, but he must not have been as strong as he looked; he couldn't budge the lid.

"Here," Mommy said, impatiently, and took the jar, and with a quick thrust, opened the lid with a loud *pop*. Aunt Beth thanked her and spooned on the strawberry compote herself.

Mommy sure was strong, Jessica Ann thought. She'd seen her do the same thing with catsup bottles and pickle jars.

"Pretty powerful for a little girl," Mark said teasingly, patting Mommy's rear end when he thought Jessica Ann couldn't see. "Remind me not to cross you."

"Don't cross me," Mommy said, and smiled her beautiful smile.

At school the next day, Jessica Ann was called to the principal's office.

But the principal wasn't there—waiting for her was the pudgy policeman, the one with the mustache. He had on a different wrinkled suit today. He didn't seem so grouchy now; he was all smiles.

"Jessica Ann?" he said, bending down. "Remember me?

I'm Lieutenant March. Could we talk for a while?"

"Okay."

"I have permission for us to use Mr. Davis' office. . . ."

Mr. Davis was the principal.

"All right."

Lt. March didn't sit at Mr. Davis' desk; he put two chairs facing each other and sat right across from Jessica Ann.

"Jessica Ann, why did your mother want to see Mrs. Withers yesterday?"

"They had a conference."

"Parent/teacher conference."

"Yes, sir."

"You don't have to call me 'sir,' Jessica Ann. I want us to be friends."

She didn't say anything.

He seemed to be trying to think of what to say next; then finally he said, "Do you know how your teacher died?"

"She fell off a ladder."

"She did fall off a ladder. But Jessica Ann—your teacher's neck was broken. . . ."

"When she fell off the ladder."

"We have a man called the Medical Examiner who says that it didn't happen that way. He says it's very likely a pair of hands did that."

Suddenly Jessica Ann remembered the jar of strawberry compote, and the other bottles and jars Mommy had twisted caps off, so easily.

"Jessica Ann . . . something was missing from Mrs. Withers' desk."

Jessica Ann's tummy started jumping.

"A plaque, Jessica Ann. A plaque for 'Outstanding Student of the Year.' You won last year, didn't you?"

"Yes, sir."

"Mrs. Withers told several friends that your mother called her, complaining about you not winning this year."

Jessica Ann said nothing.

"Jessica Ann . . . the mother of the boy who won the plaque, Eduardo's mother, Mrs. Melindez, would like to have that plaque. Means a lot to her. If you should happen to find it, would you tell me?"

"Why would *I* find it?"

"You just might. Could your mother have picked it up when she went into the classroom?"

"If she did," Jessica Ann said, "that doesn't prove anything."

"Who said anything about proving anything, Jessica Ann?"

She stood. "I think if you have any more questions for me, Lieutenant March, you should talk to my mother."

"Jessica Ann . . ."

But the little girl hear didn't hear anything else; not anything the policeman said, or what any of her friends said the rest of the day, or even the substitute teacher.

All she could hear was the sound of the lid on the strawberry compote jar popping open.

When Jessica Ann got home, she found the house empty. A note from Mommy said she had gone grocery shopping. The girl got herself some milk and cookies but neither drank nor ate. She sat at the kitchen table staring at nothing. Then she got up and began searching her mother's room.

In the middle drawer of a dresser, amid slips and panties, she found the plaque.

Her fingers flew off the object as if it were a burner on a hot stove. Then she saw her own fingerprints glowing on the brass and rubbed them off with a slick pair of panties, and put the shining plaque back, buried it in Mommy's underthings.

She went to her room and found the largest stuffed animal she could and hugged it close; the animal—a bear—had wide button eyes. So did she.

Her thoughts raced; awful possibilities presented themselves, possibilities that she may have already considered, in some corner of her mind, but had banished.

Why did Mr. Sterling die of that heart attack?

What really happened that afternoon Mommy and Daddy went boating?

She was too frightened to cry. Instead she hugged the bear and shivered as if freezing and put pieces together that fit too well. If she was right, then someone *else* she thought the world of was in danger. . . .

Mark Jeffries knew something was wrong, but he couldn't be sure what.

He and Jessica Ann had hit it off from the very start, but for the last week, whenever he'd come over to see her mother, the little girl had avoided and even snubbed him.

It had been a week since the death of Mrs. Withers—he had accompanied both Jessica Ann and her mother to the funeral—and the child had been uncharacteristically brooding ever since.

Not that Jessica Ann was ever talkative: she was a quiet child, intelligent, contemplative even, but when she opened up (as she did for Mark so often) she was warm and funny and fun.

Maybe it was because he had started to stay over at the house on occasion . . . maybe she was threatened because he had started to share her mother's bedroom. . . .

He'd been lying awake in the mother's bed, thinking these thoughts as the woman slept soundly beside him, when nature called him, and he arose, slipped on a robe and answered the call. In the hallway, he noticed the little girl's light on in her room. He stopped at the child's room and knocked, gently.

"Yes?" came her voice, softly.

"Are you awake, angel?"

"Yes."

He cracked the door. She was under the covers, wide awake, the ruffly pink shade of her nightstand lamp glowing; a stuffed bear was under there with her, hugged to her.

"What's wrong, angel?" he asked, and shut the door behind him, and sat on the edge of her bed.

"Nothing."

"You've barely spoken to me for days."

She said nothing.

"You know you're number one on my personal chart, don't you?"

She nodded.

"Do you not like my sleeping over?"

She shrugged.

"Don't you . . . don't you think I'd make a good daddy?"

Tears were welling in her eyes!

"Angel . . ."

She burst into tears, clutching him, bawling like the baby she had been, not so long ago.

"I . . . I wanted to chase you away. . . ."

"Chase me away! Why on earth . . . ?"

"Because . . . because you *would* make a good daddy, and I don't want you to die. . . ."

And she poured it all out, her fears that her mother was a murderer, that Mommy had killed her teacher and her daddy and even Mr. Sterling.

He glanced behind him at the closed door. He gently

pushed the girl away and, a hand on her shoulder, looked at her hard.

"How grown-up can you be?" he asked.

"Real grown-up, if I have to."

"Good. Because I want to level with you about something. You might be mad at me. . . ."

"Why, Mark?"

"Because I haven't been honest with you. In fact . . . I've lied. . . ."

"Lied?"

And he told her. Told her about being an investigator for the insurance company that was looking into the latest suspicious death linked to her mother, that of her stepfather, Phillip Sterling (at least, the latest one before Mrs. Withers).

Calmly, quietly, he told the little girl that he had come to believe, like her, that her mother was a murderer.

"But you . . . you slept with her. . . ."

"It's not very nice. I know. I had to get close to her, to get the truth. With your help, if you can think back and tell me about things you've seen, we might be . . ."

But that was all he got out.

The door flew open, slapping the wall like a spurned suitor, and there she was, the beautiful little blonde in the babydoll nightie, a woman with a sweet body that he hadn't been able to resist even though he knew what she most likely was.

There she was with the .38 in her hand and firing it at him, again and again; he felt the bullets hitting his body, punching him, burning into him like lasers, he thought, then one entered his right eye and put an end to all thought, and to him.

Jessica Ann was screaming, the bloody body of Mark Jeffries sprawled on the bed before her, scorched bleeding holes on the front of his robe, one of his eyes an awful black hole leaking red.

Mommy sat beside her daughter and hugged her little girl to her, slipping a hand over her mouth, stifling Jessica Ann's screams.

"Hush, dear. Hush."

Jessica Ann started to choke, and that stopped the screaming, and Mommy took her hand away. The girl looked at her mother and was startled to see tears in Mommy's eyes. She couldn't ever remember Mommy crying, not even at the funerals of Daddy and Mr. Sterling, although she had seemed to cry. Jessica Ann had always thought Mommy was faking . . . that Mommy couldn't cry . . . but now. . . .

Mommy carried Jessica Ann out of the room and down the stairs and positioned herself on the couch, with the child on her lap.

"We have to call the police, dear," she said, "and when they come, we have to tell them things that fit together. Like a puzzle fits together. Do you understand?"

"Yes, Mommy." Jessica, trembling, wanted to pull away from her mother, but somehow couldn't.

"Otherwise, Mommy will be in trouble. We don't want that, do we?"

"No, Mommy."

"Mark did bad things to Mommy. *Bedroom* things. Do you understand?"

". . . yes, Mommy."

"When I heard him in here, I thought he might be doing the same kind of things to you. Or trying to."

"But he didn't. . . ."

"That doesn't matter. And you don't have to say he did. I don't want you to lie. But those things he told you . . . about being an investigator . . . *forget* them. He never said them."

69

"Oh . . . okay, Mommy."

"If you tell, Mommy would be in trouble. We don't want that."

"No, Mommy."

"Now. Who's your best friend?"

"You . . . you are, Mommy."

"Who loves you more than anything on God's green earth?"

"You do, Mommy."

"Good girl."

There were a lot of men and women in the house, throughout the night, some of them police, in uniform, some of them in white, some in regular clothes, some using cameras, others carrying out Mark in a big black zippered bag.

Lt. March questioned Mommy for a long time; when all the others had left, he was still there, taking notes. Mommy sat on a couch in the living room, wearing a robe, her arms folded tight to her, her expression as blank as a doll's.

Aunt Beth had been called and sat with Jessica Ann in the kitchen, but there was no doorway, just an archway separating the rooms, so Jessica could see Mommy as Lt. March questioned her. Jessica Ann couldn't hear what they were saying, most of the time.

Then she saw Mommy smile at Lt. March, a funny, making-fun sort of smile, and that seemed to make Lt. March angry. He stood and almost shouted.

"No, you're not under arrest," he said, "and yes, you should contact your attorney."

He tromped out to the kitchen, to bring the empty coffee cup (Aunt Beth had given him some) and he looked very grouchy.

"Thank you," he said to Aunt Beth, handing her the cup.

"Don't you believe my sister?" Aunt Beth asked.

"Do you?" He glanced at Jessica Ann, but spoke to Aunt Beth. "I'll talk to the girl tomorrow. Maybe she should stay with you tonight."

"That's not my decision," Aunt Beth said.

"Maybe it should be," he said, and excused himself and left.

Aunt Beth looked very tired when she sat the table with Jessica Ann. She spoke quietly, almost a whisper.

"What you told me . . . is that what really happened, Jessica Ann?"

"Mommy thought Mark was going to do something bad to me."

"You love your mommy, don't you?"

"Yes."

"But you're also afraid of her."

"Yes." She shrugged. "All kids are afraid of their parents."

"Beth," Mommy said, suddenly in the archway, "you better go now."

Aunt Beth rose. She wet her lips. "Maybe I should take Jessica Ann tonight."

Mommy came over and put her hand on Jessica Ann's shoulder. "We appreciate your concern. But we've been through a lot of tragedy together, Jessica Ann and I. We'll make it through tonight, just fine. Won't we, dear?"

"Yes, Mommy."

Both Jessica Ann and her mother were questioned, separately and individually, at police headquarters in downtown Ferndale the next afternoon. Mommy's lawyer, Mr. Ekhardt, a handsome gray-haired older man, was with them; sometimes he told Mommy not to answer certain questions.

Afterward, in the hall, Jessica Ann heard Mommy ask Mr.

Ekhardt if they had enough to hold her.

"Not yet," he said. "But I don't think this is going to let up. From the looks of that lieutenant, I'd say this is just starting."

Mommy touched Mr. Ekhardt's hand with both of hers. "Thank you, Neal. With you in our corner, I'm sure we'll be just fine."

"You never give up, do you?" Mr. Ekhardt said with a funny smile. "Gotta give you that much."

Mr. Ekhardt shook his head and walked away.

Jessica Ann watched as her Mommy pulled suitcases from a closet, and then went to another closet and began packing her nicest things into one of the suitcases.

"We're going on a vacation, dear," Mommy said, folding several dresses over her arm, "to a foreign land—you'll love it there. It'll be Christmas every day."

"But I have school . . ."

"Your break starts next week, anyway. And then we'll put you in a wonderful new school."

"What about my friends?"

"You'll make new friends."

Mommy was packing so quickly, and it was all happening so fast, Jessica Ann couldn't even find the words to protest further. What could she do about it? Every kid knew that when your parents decided to move, the kid had no part of it. A kid's opinion had no weight on such matters. You just went where your parents went. . . .

"Take this," Mommy said, handing her the smaller suitcase, "and pack your own things."

"What about my animals?"

"Take your favorite. Aunt Beth will send the others on, later."

"Okay, Mommy."

"Who's your best friend?"

"You are."

"Who loves you more than . . ."

"You do."

The girl packed her bag. She put the framed picture of Daddy in the middle of the clothes, so it wouldn't get broken.

They drove for several hours. Mommy turned the radio on to a station playing that '80s music she liked—only when a love song came on, she snapped the radio off like it had done something bad to her. Now and then Mommy looked over at her, and Jessica Ann noticed Mommy's expression was . . . different. Blank, but Mommy's eyes seemed . . . was Mommy frightened, too?

When Mommy noticed Jessica Ann had caught her gaze, Mommy smiled that beautiful smile. But it wasn't real. Jessica Ann wasn't sure Mommy knew how to *really* smile.

The motel wasn't very nice. It wasn't like the Holiday Inns and Marriotts and Ramada Inns they usually stayed in on vacation. It was just a white row of doorways on the edge of some small town and a junkyard was looming in back of it, like some scary Disneyland.

Jessica Ann put on her jammies and brushed her teeth and Mommy tucked her in, even gave her a kiss. The girl was very, very tired and fell asleep quickly.

She wasn't sure how long she'd been asleep, but when she woke up, Mommy was sitting on the edge of Jessica Ann's bed. Mommy wasn't dressed for bed; she still had on the clothes she'd been driving in.

Mommy was sitting there, in the dark, staring, her hands raised in the air. It was like Mommy was trying to choke a ghost.

"Sometimes mommys have to make hard decisions,"

Mommy whispered. "If they take Mommy away, who would look after you?"

But Jessica Ann knew Mommy wasn't saying this to her, at least not to the awake her. Maybe to the sleeping Jessica Ann, only Jessica Ann wasn't sleeping. . . .

The child bolted out of the bed with a squealing scream and Mommy ran after her. Jessica Ann got to the door, which had a night latch, but her fingers fumbled with the chain, and then her mommy was on top of her. Mommy's hands were on her, but the child squeezed through, and bounded over one of the twin beds and ran into the bathroom and slammed and locked the door.

"Mommy! Mommy, don't!"

"Let me in, Jessica Ann. You just had a bad dream. Just a nightmare. We'll go back to sleep now."

"No!"

The child looked around the small bathroom and saw the window; she stood on the toilet seat lid and unlocked the window and slipped out, onto the tall grass. Behind her, she heard the splintering of the door as her mother pushed it open.

Jessica Ann was running, running toward the dark shapes that were the junkyard; she glanced back and saw her mother's face framed in the bathroom window. Her mother's eyes were wild; Jessica Ann had never seen her mother like that.

"Come back here this *instant!*" her mother said.

But Jessica Ann ran, screaming as she went, hoping to attract attention. The moon was full and high and like a spotlight on the child. Maybe someone would see!

"Help! Please, help!"

Her voice seemed to echo through the night. The other windows in the motel were dark and the highway out front was deserted; there was no one else in the world but Jessica Ann and Mommy.

And Mommy was climbing out the bathroom window.

Jessica Ann climbed over the wire fence—there was some barbed wire at the top, and her jammies got caught, and tore a little, but she didn't cut herself. Then she was on the other side, in the junkyard, but her bare feet hurt from the cinders beneath them.

Mommy was coming.

The child ran, hearing the rattle of the fence behind her, knowing Mommy was climbing, climbing over, then dropping to the other side . . .

"Jessica Ann!"

Piles of crushed cars were on either side of Jessica Ann, as she streaked down a cinder path between them, her feet hurting, bleeding, tears streaming, her crying mixed with gasping for air as she ran, ran hard as she could.

Then she fell and she skinned her knee and her yelp echoed.

She got up, quickly, and ran around the corner, and ran right into her mother.

"What do you think you're doing, young lady?"

Her mother's hands gripped the girl's shoulders.

Jessica Ann backed up quickly, bumping into a rusted-out steel drum. A wall of crushed cars, scrap metal, old tires, broken-down appliances and other things that must have had value once was behind her.

"Mommy . . ."

Mommy's hands were like claws reaching out for the girl's neck. "This is for your own good, dear. . . ."

Then Mommy's hands were on Jessica Ann's throat, and the look in Mommy's eyes was so very cold, and the child tried to cry out but she couldn't, though she tried to twist away and moonlight fell on her face.

And Mommy gazed at her child, and her eyes narrowed, and softened, and she loosened her hands.

"Put your hands *up,* Mrs. Sterling!"

Mommy stepped away and looked behind her. Jessica Ann, touching her throat where Mommy had been choking her, could see him standing there. Lt. March. He was pointing a gun at Mommy.

Mommy put her head down and her hands up.

Then Aunt Beth was there, and took Jessica Ann into her arms and held her, and said, "You're a brave little girl."

"What . . . what are you *doing* here, Aunt Beth?"

"I went along with the lieutenant. He was keeping your mother under surveillance. I'm glad you have good lungs, or we wouldn't have heard you back here. We were out front, and I'd fallen asleep. . . ."

"Aunt Beth . . . can I live with you now? I don't want to go to a new school."

Aunt Beth's laugh was surprised and sort of sad. "You can live with me. You can stay in your school." She stroked Jessica Ann's forehead. "It's over now, Jessy. It's over."

"She couldn't do it, Aunt Beth," Jessica Ann said, crying, but feeling strangely happy, somehow. Not to be rescued: but to know Mommy couldn't bring herself to do it! Mommy couldn't kill Jessica Ann!

"I know, honey," Aunt Beth said, holding the girl.

"Mommy *does* love me! More than anything on God's green earth."

The child didn't hear when Lt. March, cuffing her hands behind her, asked the woman, "Why didn't you do it? Why'd you hesitate?"

"For a moment there, in the moonlight," Mommy said, "she looked like *me.* . . ."

And the cop walked the handcuffed woman to his un-marked car, while the aunt took her niece into the motel room to retrieve a stuffed bear and a framed photo of Daddy.

MEMORIAL DAY

Flowers for Bill O'Reilly

If he hadn't been angry, Stone wouldn't have been driving so damn fast, and if he hadn't been driving so damn fast, in a lashing rain, on a night so dark closing your eyes made no difference, his high beams a pitiful pair of flashlights trying to guide the way in the vast cavern of the night, illuminating only slashes of storm, he would have had time to brake properly, when he came down over the hill and saw, in a sudden white strobe of electricity, that the bridge was gone, or anyway out of sight, somewhere down there under the rush of rain-raised river, and when the brakes didn't take, he yanked the wheel around and his Chevy coupe was sideways in a flooded ditch, wheels spinning.

Like his head.

He got out on the driver's side, because otherwise he would have had to swim underwater. From his sideways tipped car, he leapt to the slick highway, as rain pelted him mercilessly, and did a fancy slip-slide dance keeping his footing. Then he snugged the wings of the trenchcoat collar up around his face and began to walk back the way he'd come. If rain was God's tears, the Old Boy sure was bawling about something tonight.

Private detective Richard Stone had spent the afternoon in the upstate burg of Hopeful, only there was nothing hopeful about the sorry little hamlet. All he'd wanted was to do a kindness for an old lady, and find a few answers to a few questions. Like how a guy who won a Silver Star charging up a beachhead could wind up a crushed corpse in a public park, a crumpled piece of discarded human refuse.

Bill O'Reilly had had his problems. Before the war he'd been an auto mechanic on the Northside. A good-looking dark-haired bruiser who'd have landed a football scholarship at Notre Dame if the war hadn't got in the way, he married his high school sweetheart before he shipped out, only when he came back missing an arm and a leg, he found his girl wasn't interested in what was left of him. Even though he was pretty good with that prosthetic arm and leg of his, he couldn't get his job back at the garage, either.

Stone and O'Reilly weren't friends, exactly. It was more like, friend of a friend. The detective knew the slightly younger man through Katie Crockett, secretary at Stone Investigations (and Stone's fiancée); Bill had been a good friend of Katie's late brother, Ben, who died in the war.

And Stone himself, though at six feet a fairly strapping physical specimen, had not gone to war. Due to his bone fide detective's flat feet, Stone had been classified 4-F. He didn't feel particularly guilty about that—at least, he didn't admit it to himself, if he did.

Not so long ago, Katie, sitting in Stone's lap in his inner office, not exactly taking dictation, had said, "Please help Bill out. Help him find work. He gave so much . . ."

"And I didn't?"

"That's not how I meant it, Richard . . . but you didn't, did you? Boys like Ben and him made such a sacrifice for their country . . ."

"You mind not using my lap for a soapbox?"

Katie's pretty mouth tightened and she got to her feet, sandy hair flouncing. She said curtly, "I don't mind not using your lap at all, for anything."

79

And she had skirt-swishingly clip-clopped her high-heeled way back out into the reception area.

So Stone had tried to help O'Reilly out, he had really tried, only Bill—a great guy, a regular Joe—had brought back more from the war than just a Silver Star and disabilities; he'd also carried home nightmares, and recurrences of malaria, and a growing tendency to drown his troubled memories in a bottle.

But the last time Stone had spoken to O'Reilly, when they'd gone to catch Goliath Murphy take on Jersey Joe at the arena, an on-the-wagon Bill had said things were looking up. Said he had a handyman job lined up in a little town up-state—Hopeful, where as kid he used to visit a maiden aunt, and where he'd spent so many summers it was like a second home to him, even to where he was known around town, and remembered fondly. This was a chance to go home again, and start over, plus the position was going to pay better than his old job at the garage.

"Besides which," he said, between rounds, "you oughta see my boss. You'd do overtime yourself."

"What kind of boss is that?"

"The kind of boss that's easy on the peepers."

Jersey Joe whammed Goliath a good one and the crowd moaned in collective disappointment; Stone had to work his voice up over the din to get in, "What, are you working for a woman?"

Bill nodded, grinning. "And what a woman."

The crowd was settling down and Bill didn't have to work as hard as Stone had to be heard. "She's got more curves than a mountain road."

Stone arched an eyebrow. "Easy you don't drive off a cliff."

That's all they'd said about the subject, because Goliath

had come out swinging at that point, the arena crowd roaring, and the next Stone heard from Bill—well not from him, about him—he was dead.

It was the morning after Memorial Day when the call came in, a collect call from an Agnes O'Reilly.

"Operator," Stone had said, "I'm afraid I don't know any Agnes O'Reilly . . ."

But Katie had come scooting in, saying urgently, "That's Bill's aunt!"

Stone, cupping the receiver, gave his cute secretary a wry grin. "Eavesdropping again, baby?"

Mild embarrassment passed over the pretty face, but she said only, "You don't get that many long distance calls," and pulled up the dictation chair and waited for him to do the right thing.

"I'll accept the charges, operator," Stone said.

The voice was quavery, the connection staticky; you would have thought the call was from the next world and not forty miles north of Chicago.

"Thank you, thank you, Mr. Stone, for taking this call. Bill had your number in his wallet, but I didn't have an address or would have written . . . wouldn't have troubled you with this expense. . . ."

The old girl was weeping through all this.

"What is it, Miss O'Reilly? Has there been an accident?"

"They say there has. They say it was a car."

"Is Bill all right?"

"No . . . no. He's dead, Mr. Stone. After all he survived overseas, and now he's dead."

"I'm very sorry. Can you talk about it, Miss O'Reilly?"

Gradually, he was able to get it out of her. Bill's body had been found in Hopeful's city park. His spine had been snapped.

"I couldn't . . . couldn't afford to bury him properly, Mr.

81

Stone. All those beautiful flowers yesterday in the Hopeful cemetery . . . 'Taps' playing . . . American flags flying. . . . I could see it from my window . . . such a lovely ceremony. But not for Bill."

Katie was crying into a hanky; even from only one side of the phone conversation, she could gather what had happened.

"I wish we'd known, Miss O'Reilly," Stone said. "We'd have come to the funeral. There'd have been flowers."

"There was no funeral, Mr. Stone. I'm so ashamed. I have no money. He was buried in a pauper's grave."

Stone swallowed, shifted in his swivel chair. "I'm sorry. Is there anything I can do?"

"No. No, there's nothing anything any of us can do for Bill except . . . pray. Pray he's at rest and safely in the Lord's bosom. I knew you were Bill's friend. He spoke so highly of you. So I thought you should know."

Stone thanked Bill's aunt, and soon he was holding the tearful Katie in his arms.

"You have to go there, Richard. Right now!"

"Well . . . what is there to do about this, baby? Bill's dead. Tracking down hit-and-run drivers, that's police business. . . ."

She drew away from him slightly and looked at him, her lovely lips quivering. "I want you to claim the body."

"What? Hell, Katie, he's already buried!"

"In a pauper's grave, you said. He was a hero, Richard. It's not right."

He sighed. "I know. We'd could have gotten him into Arlington, if his aunt had only thought to call me sooner."

Her expression was firm. "I want him buried next to Ben. In St. Simon's cemetery. Next Memorial Day, there will be flowers for Bill O'Reilly."

★ ★ ★ ★ ★

Chief Thadeous Dolbert was one of Hopeful's four full-time cops. Despite his high office, he wore a blue uniform indistinguishable from his underlings, and his desk was out in the open of the little bullpen in the storefront-style police station. A two-cell lock-up was against one wall, and Spring sunshine streaming in the windows through the bars sent slanting stripes of shadow across his desk and his fat florid face.

Dolbert was leaning back in his swivel chair, eyes hooded; he looked like a fat iguana—Stone expected his tongue to flick out and capture a fly any second now.

Stone said, "How does a thing like that happen, Chief?"

Dolbert said, "We figure he got hit by a car."

"Body was found in the city park, wasn't it?"

The chief nodded slowly. "Way he was bunged up, figure he must've got whopped a good one, really sent him flyin'."

"Was that the finding at the inquest?"

Dolbert fished a pack of cigarettes out of his breast pocket, right behind his tarnished badge; lighted himself up a smoke. Soon it was dangling from a thick slobber-flecked lower lip.

"We don't stand much on ceremony around here, Mr. Stone. County coroner called it accidental death at the scene."

"That's all the investigation Bill's death got?"

Dolbert shrugged, blew a smoke circle. "All that was warranted."

Stone sat forward. "All that was warranted. A guy who gave an arm and a leg to his country, wins a damn Silver Star doing it, and you figure him getting his spine snapped like a twig and damn near every bone in his body broken, well that's just pretty much business as usual here in Hopeful."

Under the heavy lids, fire flared in the fat chief's eyes but his voice and demeanor remained calm. "I knew Bill O'Reilly

83

when he was a kid; me and my brother and him used to go swimming out to the gravel pits. Nice kid, Bill . . . But that was the old Bill. Not the drunken stumblebum he turned into."

"I just saw him a month or so ago, and he was on the wagon."

"Well, he fell the hell off, then. That lush was a prime candidate for stepping out in front of a car."

Stone held his irritation in; he needed this fat jackass's cooperation. "You make any effort to find the hit-and-run driver that did this?"

The chief shrugged. "Nobody saw it happen."

"You don't even know for sure a car did it."

"How the hell else could it have happened?"

Stone shrugged one shoulder, smiled ever so slightly. "Maybe I'll just take a little time here in your fair city, and find out."

A finger as thick as a pool cue waggled at the detective. "You got no business stickin' your damn nose in around here, Stone—"

"I'm a licensed investigator in this state, Chief. And I'm working for Bill O'Reilly's aunt."

Dolbert snorted a laugh. "Working for that senile old biddy? She's out at the county hospital. She's broke! Couldn't even afford a damn funeral . . . we had to bury the boy in potter's field. . . ."

That was one of Hopeful's claims to fame: the state buried its unknown, unclaimed, impoverished dead, in the potter's field there.

"Why didn't you tell Uncle Sam?" Stone demanded. "Bill was a war hero—they'd've buried him with honors. . . ."

Dolbert shrugged. "Not my job."

"What the hell is your job?"

84

"Watch your mouth, city boy." He nodded toward the holding cells and the cigarette quivered as the fat mouth sneered. "You may be big shit in the big town—but don't forget you're in my world now. . . ."

Stone stood up, pushed back, the legs of his wooden chair scraping the hard floor like fingernails on a blackboard.

"Good," Stone said calmly. "Then you're just the man I need." He slapped the chief's desk and papers and other junk on it jumped. "I'm here to reclaim Bill's body. He's going to get a proper burial, in the 'big town.' Put the paperwork in motion and I'll get back with you."

The chief seemed suddenly flustered. "Well, hell, that just ain't done. . . . I mean, he's dead and buried. . . . You'll have me swimmin' in red tape. . . ."

From the doorway, Stone said, "What's the problem with that? You can swim. Remember you and Bill out at the gravel pits?"

And Stone left the storefront police station, not quite slamming the door. On the sidewalk, he looked out on an idyllic small town scene that might have emerged from the brush of Norman Rockwell—sunshine dappling the lawn of the stately courthouse in the town square, ladies shopping, farmers loading up supplies, lazily flapping flags commemorating the war dead who yesterday the town had honored at the Hopeful cemetery, where Bill O'Reilly had received neither flowers nor gravestone.

But Bill was going to get a memorial, all right—by way of a Richard Stone investigation.

Only nobody in Hopeful wanted to talk to the detective. The supposed "accident" had occurred in the middle of the night, and Stone's only chance for a possible witness was in the all-night diner across from the Civil War cannon in the park.

The diner's manager, a skinny character with a horsy face darkened by perpetual five o'clock shadow, wore a grease-stained apron over his grease-stained T-shirt. Like the chief, he had a cigarette drooping from slack lips. The ash narrowly missed falling into the cup of coffee he'd served Stone, who sat at the counter among half a dozen locals.

"We got a jukebox, mister," the manager said. "Lots of kids end up here, tail end of a Saturday night. That was a Saturday night, when Bill got it, ya know? That loud music, joint jumpin', there coulda been a train wreck out there and nobody'da heard it."

Stone was nibbling at a cheeseburger and fries. "Nobody would have seen an accident, out your windows?"

The manager shrugged. "Maybe ol' Bill got hit on the other side of the park."

Stone craned his neck around. The "park" was just a little square of grass and benches and such; the "other side of the park" was easily visible from the windows lining the diner booths—even factoring in the grease and lettering.

"Seems to me it'd be pretty hard to miss it from here," Stone said, "even across the park."

"Nights get pretty dark around these parts."

"No kidding?" Stone asked, filing that one away as the dumbest response to a question he'd ever received.

Next, the detective talked to a couple of waitresses, who claimed not to have been working that night. One of them, "Gladys" her nametag said, a heavyset bleached blonde who must have been pretty cute twenty years ago, served Stone a slice of apple pie with cheese and a piece of information.

Stone forked a bite of pie, lifted it to his mouth and said casually, "Bill told me he was going to work as a handyman, for some good-lookin' gal. You know who that would've been?"

"Sure," Gladys said. She had sky-blue eyes and nicotine-yellow teeth. "He was working out at the mansion."

"The what?"

"The mansion. The old Riddle place. You must've passed it on Back Country highway, comin' in to town."

Remembering, Stone nodded. "I did see a gate and a drive, and got a glimpse of a big old gothic brick barn. . . ."

She nodded, refilled his coffee. "That's the one. The Riddles, they owned this town forever. Ain't a building downtown that the Riddles ain't owned since the dawn of time. But Mr. Riddle, he was the last of the line, and him and his wife died in that plane crash, oh, ten years ago. The only one left now is the daughter—Victoria."

"What was Bill doing out at the Riddle place?"

She shrugged. "Who knows? Who cares? Maybe Miz Riddle just wanted some company. Bill was a handsome so and so, even minus a limb or two." She sighed, her expression turning wistful. "He coulda put his shoe under my bed anytime."

"This Victoria Riddle—she's a looker, then?"

Gladys rolled her eyes. "A real knockout. Like a movie star. Imagine getting born with that kinda silver spoon—money *and* looks."

"And she isn't married? She lives alone?"

"Alone except for that hairless ape."

Stone put his fork down. "What?"

"She's got a sort of butler, you know, a servant? He was her father's chauffeur. Big guy. Mute. Comes in to town, does the grocery shopping and such. We hardly ever see Miz Riddle, 'less she's meeting with her lawyer, or going to the bank to visit all her money."

"What does she do out there?"

"Who knows? She's not interested in business. Her daddy,

he had his finger in every pie around here. Miz Riddle, she lets her lawyer run things and I guess the family money, uh, under-what's-it? Underwrites, is that the word?"

"I guess."

"Underwrites her research."

"Research?"

"Oh, yeah. Miz Riddle's a doctor."

"Medical doctor?"

"Sort of, but not the kind that hangs out a shingle. She's some kind of scientific genius."

"So she's doing medical research out there?"

"I guess." She shook her head. "Pity about Bill. Such a nice fella."

"Had he been drinking heavy?"

"Bill? Naw. Oh, he liked a drink. I suppose he shut his share of bars down on a Saturday night, but he wasn't no alcoholic. Not like that other guy."

"What other guy?"

Her expression turned distant. "Funny."

The back of Stone's neck was tingling. "What's funny? What other guy?"

"Not funny ha ha. Funny weird. That other guy, don't remember his name, just some tramp who come through, he was a crip, too."

"A crip?"

"Yeah. He had one arm. Guess he lost his in the war, too. He was working out at the Riddle mansion, as a handyman—one-handed handyman. That guy, he really was a drunk."

"What became of him?"

"That's what's funny weird. Three, four months ago, he wound up like Bill. They found him in the gutter on Main Street, all bunged up, deader than a bad battery. Hit and run victim—just like Bill."

★ ★ ★ ★ ★

The wrought-iron gate in the gray-brick wall stood open and Stone tooled the Chevy coupe up a winding red-brick drive across a gentle treeless slope where the sprawling gabled tan-brick gothic mansion crouched like a lion about to pounce. The golf-course of a lawn had its own rough behind the house, a virtual forest preserve that seemed at once to shelter and encroach upon the stark lines of the house.

Steps led to an open cement pedestal of a porch with a massive slab of a wooden door where Stone had a choice between an ornate iron knocker and a simple doorbell. He rang the bell.

He stood there listening to birds chirping and enjoying the cool breeze that seemed to whisper rain was on its way, despite the golden sunshine reflecting off the lawn. Then he rang the bell again.

Stone was about to go around back, to see if there was another door he could try, when that massive slab of wood creaked open like the start of the "Inner Sanctum" radio program; the three-hundred-and-fifty pound apparition who stood suddenly before him would have been at home on a spook show, himself.

He was six four, easy, towering over Stone's rangy six; he wore the black uniform of a chauffeur, but no cap, his tie a loose black string thing. He looked like an upended Buick with a person painted on it. His head was the shape of a grape and just as hairless, though considerably larger; he had no eyebrows either, wide, bulging eyes, a lump of a nose and an open mouth.

"Unnggh," he said.

"I'd like to see Miss Riddle," Stone said.

"Unnggh," he said.

"It's about Bill O'Reilly. I represent his family. I'm here to ask some questions."

His brow furrowed in something approaching thought.

Then he slammed the door in Stone's face.

Normally, Stone didn't put up with crap like that. He'd been polite, and the butler had been rude. Kicking the door in, and the butler's teeth, was what seemed called for. Only this boy was a walking side of beef that gave even a hardcase like Richard Stone pause.

And Stone was, in fact, pausing, wondering whether to ring the bell again, go around back, or just climb in his coupe and drive the hell away, when the door opened again and the human Buick was replaced by a human goddess.

She was tall, standing eye to eye with the detective, and though she wore a loose-fitting white lab jacket that hung low over a simple black dress, nylons and flat shoes, those mountain-road curves Bill had mentioned were not easily hidden. Her dark blonde hair was tied back, and severe black-frame glasses rode the perfect little nose; she wore almost no make-up, perhaps just a hint of lipstick, or was that the natural color of those full lips? Whatever effort she'd made to conceal her beauty behind a mask of scientific sterility was futile: the big green eyes, the long lashes, the high cheekbones, the creamy complexion, that full-high-breasted, wasp-waisted, long-limbed figure, all conspired to make her as stunning a female creature as God had ever created.

"I'm sorry," she said, in a silky contralto. "This is a private residence and a research center. We see no one without an appointment."

"The gate was open."

"We're expecting the delivery of certain supplies this evening," she said, "and I leave the gate standing open on such occasions. You see, I'm short-handed. But why am I boring you with this? Good afternoon. . . ."

And the door began to close.

He held it open with the flat of his hand. "My name is Richard Stone."

The green eyes narrowed. "The detective?"

He smiled. "You must get the city papers up here."

Several of Stone's cases had hit the headlines.

"We do," she said. "Hopeful isn't the end of the world."

"It was for Bill O'Reilly."

Her expression softened, and she cracked the door open, wider. "Poor Bill. Were you a friend?"

"Yes."

"So you've come to ask about his death."

"That's right." Stone shrugged. "I am a detective."

"Of course," she said, opening the door. "And you're looking into the circumstances. A natural way for you to deal with such a loss. . . ."

She gestured for him to enter, and Stone followed her through a high-ceilinged entryway. The hairless ape appeared like an apparition and took his trenchcoat; Stone kept his fedora, but took it off, out of deference to his hostess.

In front of him, a staircase led to a landing, then to a second floor; gilt-framed family portraits lined the way. On one side was a library with more leather in bindings and chairs than your average cattle herd; on the other was a formal sitting room where elegant furnishings that had been around long enough to become antiques were overseen by a glittering chandelier.

She led Stone to a rear room and it was as if, startlingly, they'd entered a penthouse apartment—the paintings on the wall were remarkably abstract and modern, and the furnishings were, too, with a hi-fi console and a zebra wet bar with matching stools; but the room was original with the house, or at least the fireplace and mantle indicated as much. Over the fireplace was the only artwork in the room that wasn't abstract: a full-length portrait of his hostess in a low-cut evening gown, a painting that was impossibly lovely with no exaggeration on the part of the artist.

She slipped out of her lab coat, tossing it on a boomerang of a canvas chair, revealing a short-sleeve white blouse providing an understated envelope for an overstated bosom. Undoing her hair, she allowed its length to shimmer to her shoulders. The severe black-framed glasses, however, she left in place.

Her walk was as liquid as mercury in a vial as she got behind the bar and poured herself a martini. "Fix you a drink?"

"Got any beer back there?"

"Light or dark?"

"Dark."

They sat on a metal-legged couch that shouldn't have been comfortable but was; she was sipping a martini, her dark nyloned legs crossed, displaying well-developed calves. For a scientist, she made a hell of a specimen.

Stone sipped his beer—it was a bottle of German imported stuff, a little bitter for his taste, but very cold.

"That's an interesting butler you have there," Stone said.

"I have to apologize for Bolo," she said, stirring the cocktail with her speared olive. "His tongue was cut out by natives in the Amazon."

"Ouch," Stone said.

"My father was on an exploratory trip, somehow incurred the wrath of the natives, and Bolo interceded on his behalf. By offering himself, in the native custom, Bolo bought my father's life—but paid with his tongue."

With a kiss-like bite, she plucked the olive from its spear and chewed.

"He doesn't look much like a South American native," Stone said.

"He isn't. He was a Swedish missionary. My father never told me Bolo's real name . . . but that was what the natives called him."

"And I don't suppose Bolo's told you, either."

A smile flickered on the full lips. "No. But he can communicate. He can write. In English. His mental capacity seems somewhat diminished, but he understands what's said to him."

"Very kind of you to keep somebody like that around."

"Like what?"

He shrugged. "Handicapped."

"Mr. Stone . . ."

"Make it Richard—and I'll call you Victoria. Or do you prefer Vicki?"

"How do you know I don't prefer 'Doctor'?"

Stone offered up another shrug. "Hey, it's okay with me. I played doctor before."

"Are you flirting with me, Richard?"

"I might be."

"Or you might be trying to get me to let my guard down."

"Why—is it up?"

She glanced at his lap. "You tell me."

Now Stone crossed his legs. "Where's your research lab?"

"In back."

"Sorry if I'm interrupting . . ."

She shook her head, no, and the dark blonde hair shimmered some more. "I'm due for a break. I'd like to help you, Mr. Stone—Richard. You see, I thought a lot of Bill. He worked hard. He may not have been the brightest guy around, but he made up for it with enthusiasm and energy. Some people let physical limitations get in their way. Not Bill."

"You must have a thing for taking in strays."

"What do you mean?"

Stone waved a hand. "Well . . . like Bolo. Like Bill. I understand you took in another handicapped veteran, not so long ago."

"That's right. George Wilson." She shook her head sadly. "Such a shame. He was a hard worker, too—"

"He died the same way as Bill."

"I know."

"Doesn't that strike you as . . . a little odd? Overly coincidental?"

"Richard, George was a heavy drinker, and Bill was known to tie one on, himself. It may seem 'coincidental,' but I'm sure they aren't the first barroom patrons to wobble into the street after closing and get hit by a car."

Stone raised an eyebrow. "Nobody saw either one of them get hit by a car."

"Middle of the night. These things happen."

"Not twice. Not in a flyspeck like Hopeful."

The green eyes narrowed with interest and concern. "What do you think happened, Richard?"

"I have no idea—yet. But I'll say this—everybody seemed to like Bill. I talked to a lot of people today, and nobody, except maybe the police chief, had an unkind word to say about Bill. So I'm inclined to think the common factors between Bill and this George Wilson hold the answer. Frankly—you're one of those common factors."

She touched her bosom. "But surely not the only one."

"Hardly. They were both war veterans, down on their luck."

"No shortage of those."

"And they were both handicapped."

She nodded, apparently considering these facts, scientist that she was. "Are you staying in Hopeful tonight?"

"No. I have a court appearance in the city tomorrow. I'll be back on the weekend. Poke around some more."

She put a hand on his thigh. "If I think of anything, how can I find you?"

Stone patted the hand, removed it, stood. "Keep your gate open," he said, slipping on his fedora, "and I'll find you."

She licked her lips; they glistened. "I'll make sure I leave my gate wide open, on Saturday."

He laughed. "You flirting with me, doctor?"

"I might be. Must I call you 'Richard'?"

"Why?"

"I think I might prefer 'Dick.' "

Stone was still contemplating Victoria's final double-entendre as under a darkening sky, he tooled back into Hopeful, to talk to the nightshift at the diner. He got nowhere for his efforts and headed toward the city, in the downpour, annoyed at how little he'd learned. Now, with his car in the ditch, and rain lashing down relentlessly, he found himself back at the Riddle mansion well before Saturday. The gate was still open, though—she must not have received that delivery of supplies she'd talked about, yet.

Splashing through puddles on the winding drive, he kept his trenchcoat collar snugged around him as he headed toward the towering brick house. In the daytime, the mansion had seemed striking, a bit unusual; on this black night, illuminated momentarily in occasional flashes of lightning, its gothic angles were eerily abstract, the planes of the building a stark ghostly white.

This time he used the knocker, hammering with it. It wasn't all that late—maybe nine o'clock or a little after. But it felt like midnight and instinctively Stone felt the need to wake the dead.

Bolo answered the door. The lights in the entryway were out and he was just a big black blot, distinguishable only by that upended Buick shape of his; then the world turned white, him along with it, and when the thunder caught up with the lightning, Stone damn near jumped.

"Tell your mistress Mr. Stone's back," he said. "My car's in a ditch and I need—"

That's when the son of a bitch slammed the door in Stone's face. Second time that day. A flush of anger started to rise up around the detective's collar but it wasn't drying him off, even if the shelter of the awning over the slab of porch was keeping him from getting wetter. Only Stone wasn't sure a human being could be any wetter than he was, right now.

When the door opened again, he drew back a fist to let that big bastard have it—only the figure standing there was Victoria.

She wore a red silk robe, belted tight around her tiny waist. The sheen of the robe and the folds of the silk conspired with her curves to create a dizzying display of pulchritude.

"Mr. Stone . . . Richard! Come in, come in."

He did. The light in the entryway was on now, and Bolo was there again, taking Stone's drenched hat and coat. Even without them, he formed puddles at his feet as he quickly explained to her what had happened.

"With this storm," she said, "and the bridge out, you'll need to stay the night."

"Love to," he said. Mother Stone didn't raise any fools.

"But you'll have to get out of those wet things," she continued. "I think I have an old nightshirt of my father's. . . ."

She took him back to that ultra-modern sitting room and Stone was soon in her father's nightshirt, swathed in blankets, sitting before the fireplace's glow, its magical flickering soothingly restful, and making her portrait above the fire seem alive, smiling seductively, the bosom in the low-cut gown seemingly heaving with passion.

Shaking his head, wondering if he'd completely lost his sanity, Stone tucked Sadie—his best girl, which was to say, his trusty .38—behind a pillow. Hardware like that could be distressing to the gentle sensibilities of some females.

When she cracked the door to ask if he was decent, Stone said, "That's one thing I've never been accused of, but come on in."

Then she was sitting next to him, the red silk gown playing delightful reflective games with the firelight.

"Can I tell you something terrible?" she asked, like a child with an awful secret.

"I hope you will."

"I'm glad your car went in the ditch."

"And here I thought you liked me."

"I do," she said, and she edged closer. "That's why I'm glad."

She seemed to want him to kiss her, so he did, and it was a long, deep kiss, hotter than the fire, wetter than the night, and then his hands were on top of the smoothness of the silk gown. And then they were on the smoothness underneath it. . . .

"There's a guest room upstairs," she said huskily, into his ear.

"This is fine right here," he said, easing away from her, wanting to pursue this but reminding himself he was engaged to Katie—though, goddamnit, it was her idea he take this case, wasn't it?

But there was something wrong here aside from running around on Katie. Stone was well aware that his dark good looks had made him popular with the ladies; but usually not this popular, this fast. . . .

"I'll just couch it," he said. "Anyway, I like the fire."

Victoria slipped from his arms, floated off the couch like sexy smoke and soon was making herself a drink behind the bar, and got him another German beer.

She handed him the bottle of beer, its cold wetness in his palm contrasting with the warmth of the room, and the moment. Sitting next to him, close to him, she sipped her drink.

"First thing tomorrow," she said, "we'll call into town for a tow truck, and get your car pulled out of that ditch."

"No hurry."

Her brow lifted. "Don't you have a court appearance to-morrow?"

"Even judges consider acts of God a good excuse," he said, and rested the beer on an amoeba-shaped coffee table nearby, then leaned in and kissed her again. Just a friendly peck.

"Aren't you thirsty?" she asked, nodding toward the beer.

Why was she so eager for him to drink that brew?

He said, "Dry as a bone," and reached for the bottle, lifted it to his lips, and seemed to take a drink.

Seemed to.

Now she gave Stone a friendly kiss, said, "See you at breakfast," and rose, sashaying out as she cinched the silk robe back up. If she could bottle that walk, he thought, she'd really have something worth researching.

Alone, he sniffed the beer. His unscientific brain couldn't

detect anything, but he knew damn well it contained a mickey. She wanted him to sleep through this night. He didn't know why, but something was going to happen here that a houseguest like Stone—even one who'd been lulled into a false sense of security by a very giving hostess—shouldn't see.

So he poured the bottle of beer down the drain and quickly went to the couch and got himself under the blankets and pretended to be asleep.

But Stone couldn't have been more alert if he'd been walking a tightrope. His eyes only seemed shut; they were slitted open and saw her when she peeked in to see if he was sleeping. He even saw her mouth and eyes tighten in smug satisfaction before the door closed, followed by the click of locking him in. . . .

The rain was still sheeting down when, wearing only her daddy's nightshirt, Stone went out a window and, Sadie in hand, found his way to the back of the building where a new section had been added on, institutional-looking brick with no windows at all. The thin cotton cloth of the nightshirt was a transparent second skin by the time he found his way around the building and discovered an open double garage, also back behind, following an extension of the original driveway. The garage doors stood open and a single vehicle—a panel truck bearing the Hopeful Police Department insignia—was within, dripping with water, as if it were sweating.

Cautiously, Stone slipped inside, grateful to be out of the rain. Along the walls of the garage were various boxes and crates with medical supply house markings. He could hear approaching footsteps and ducked behind a stack of crates.

Peeking out, he could see Chief Dolbert, in a rain slicker and matching hat, leading the way for Bolo, still in his chauffeur-type uniform. Dolbert opened up the side of the van and Bolo leaned in.

And when Bolo leaned back out, he had his arms filled with a person, a woman—in fact, a naked one!

Then Bolo walked away from the panel truck, toward the door back into the building, held open for him by the thoughtful police chief. It was as if Bolo were carrying a bride across the threshold.

Only this bride was dead.

For ten minutes Stone watched as Bolo made trips from the building to the panel truck, where with the chief's assistance he conveyed naked dirt-smeared dead bodies into the house. Stone's mind reeled with the unadorned horror of it: Norman Rockwell had given way suddenly to Hieronymous Bosch.

Richard Stone was shivering, and not just from the water-soaked nightshirt he was in.

Somehow, being in that nightshirt, naked under it, made him feel a kinship to these poor dead bastards, many of them desiccated-looking souls, with unkempt hair and bony ill-fed bodies, and finally it came to him.

Stone knew who these poor dead wretches were. And he knew why, at least roughly why, Chief Dolbert was delivering them, the "supplies" Victoria had been awaiting.

When at last the doors on the panel truck were shut, and the ghastly delivery complete, the chief and Bolo headed back into the building. That pleased Stone—he was afraid the chief would take off into the rainy, thunderous night, and didn't want him to.

Stone wanted Dolbert around.

Not long after they had disappeared into the building, Stone went in after them.

And into hell.

It was a blindingly well-illuminated hell, a white and silver hell, resembling a hospital operating room but much larger, a hell dominated by the silver of surgical instruments, a hell where the walls were lined with knobs and dials and meters and gizmos, a hell dominated by naked corpses on metal autopsy-type tables, their empty eyes staring at the bright overhead lighting.

And the seductive Satan who ruled over this hell, Victoria Riddle, who was back in her lab coat now, hair tucked in a bun, was filling the open palm of Chief Dolbert with greenbacks.

But where was Bolo?

Stone glanced over his shoulder, and there the butler was, tucked behind the door, standing like a cigar store Indian, awaiting his mistress' next command, only she didn't have to give this command: Bolo knew enough to reach out for this intruder, his hands clawed, his eyes bulging to where the whites showed all around, his mouth open in a soundless snarl.

"Stop!" Stone told the looming figure, which threw his shadow over the detective like a blue blanket.

But Bolo didn't stop.

And when Stone squeezed Sadie's trigger and Sadie blew the top of Bolo's bald head off, splashing the white wall behind him with the colors of the inside of the butler's head, red and gray and white, making another abstract painting only without a frame, that didn't stop him either, didn't stop him from falling on top of Stone, and by the time Stone had pushed his massive dead weight off, the fat corpse emptying ooze out the top of the bald blown-off skull, he had another fat bastard to deal with, a live one: the chief of the Hopeful police department, whose revolver pointed down at Stone.

"Drop it," Dolbert said.

The chief should have just shot Stone, because the detective took advantage of Dolbert taking time to speak and shot him, in the head, and the gun in the chief's hand was useless now, since his brain could no longer send it signals, and the fat former police chief toppled back on top of one of the corpses, sharing its silver tray, staring up at the ceiling, the red hole in his forehead like an extra expressionless eye.

"You fool," Victoria said, the lovely face lengthening into a contorted ugly mask, green eyes wild behind the glasses.

"I decided I wasn't thirsty after all," Stone said, as he weaved his way between the corpses on their metal slabs.

"You don't understand! This is serious research! This will benefit humanity. . . ."

"I understand you were paying the chief for fresh cadavers," Stone said. "With him in charge of the state's potter's field, you had no shortage of dead guinea pigs. But what I don't understand is, why kill Bill, and George Wilson, when you had access to all these riches?"

And Stone gestured to the deceased indigents around them.

Her face eased back into beauty; her scientific mind had told her, apparently, that her best bet now was to try to reason with the detective. Calmly. Coolly.

Stone was close enough to her to kiss her, only now he didn't feel much like kissing her and, anyway, the .38 he was aiming at her belly would have been in the way of an embrace.

"George Wilson tried to blackmail me," she said. "Bill . . . Bill just wouldn't cooperate. He said he was going to the authorities."

"About your ghoulish arrangement with the chief, you mean?"

She nodded. Then earnestness coated her voice:

"Richard, I was only trying to help Bill, and George—and mankind. Don't you see? I wanted to make them whole again!"

"Oh my God," Stone said, getting it. "Bill was a live guinea pig, wasn't he? Wilson, too. . . ."

Her head tilted back in a gesture that was both proud and defensive. "That's not how I'd express it, exactly, but yes. . . ."

"You wanted to make them living Frankenstein monsters . . . you wanted to sew the limbs of the dead on 'em. . . ."

Her eyes lighted up with enthusiasm, and hope. "Yes! Yes! With the correct tissue matches, and my own research into electro-chemical transplant techniques . . ."

That was when the lights went out.

God's electricity had killed man's electricity, and the cannon roar aftermath of the thunderbolt wasn't enough to hide the sound of her scurrying in the dark amongst the trays of the dead, trying to escape, heading for that door onto the garage.

Stone went after her, but she had knowledge of the layout of the place and he didn't, the detective kept bumping into bodies, and then she screamed.

Just for a split second.

A hard whump had interrupted the scream, and before Stone even had time to wonder what the hell had happened, the lights came back on, and there she was.

On her back, on the floor, her head resting against the metal underbar of one of the dead-body trays, only resting wasn't really the word, since she'd hit hard enough to crack open her skull and a widening pool of red was forming below her head as she too stared up at the ceiling with wide-open eyes, just another corpse in a roomful of corpses. Bolo's dead body, where Stone had pushed his dead weight off of him, was—as was fitting—at his mistress' feet.

Stone grimaced.

Bolo may not have had many brains in that chrome dome of his, but he'd had enough to slip her up.

They didn't wait for the next Memorial Day to come around. Stone and Katie stood close together, the detective's arm around the pretty girl's slender waist, and admired the flowers on the fresh grave in St. Simon's cemetery. Fall wind whispered through Katie's red-tinged locks and ruffled and rustled the many-colored flowers.

The old lady in the wheelchair, on a rare afternoon outing from the county hospital in Hopeful, was dabbing tears from eyes in a face that reminded Stone of his late friend; but the old girl, for all her tears, was smiling.

FATHER'S DAY

His Father's Ghost

The bus dropped him off at a truck stop two miles from Greenwood, and Jeff had milk and homemade cherry pie before walking the two miles to the little town. It was May, a sunny cool afternoon that couldn't make up its mind whether to be spring or summer, and the walk along the blacktop up and over rolling hills was pleasant enough.

On the last of these hills—overlooking where the undulating Grant Wood farmland flattened out to nestle the small collection of houses and buildings labeled "Greenwood" by a water tower—was the cemetery. The breeze riffled the leaves of trees that shaded the gravestones; it seemed to Jeff that someone was whispering to him, but he couldn't make out what they were saying.

Nobody rich buried here; no fancy monuments, anyway. He stopped at the top and worked his way down. The boy— Jeff was barely twenty-one—in his faded jeans and new running shoes and Desert Storm sweatshirt, duffel bag slung over his arm, walked backward, eyes slowly scanning the names. When he reached the bottom, he began back up the hill, still scanning, and was threading his way down again when he saw the name.

Carl Henry Hastings—Beloved Husband, Loving Father. 1954-1992.

Jeff Carson studied the gravestone; put his hand on it. Ran

his hand over the chiseled inscription. He thought about dropping to his knees, for a prayer. But he couldn't, somehow. He'd been raised religious—or anyway, Methodist—but he didn't have much faith in any of that, anymore.

And he couldn't feel what he wanted to feel; he felt as dead as those around him. As cold inside as the marble of the tombstone.

The wind was whispering to him, through the trees, but he still couldn't make out what was being said to him, and just walked on into the little town, stopping at a motel just beyond the billboard announcing "New Jersey's Cleanest Little City" and a sign marking the city limits and population (6000).

He tapped the bell on the counter to summon a woman he could see in a room back behind there, to the right of the wall of keys, in what seemed to be living quarters, watching a soap opera, the volume so loud it was distorting. Maybe she didn't want to hear the bell.

But she heard it anyway, a heavy-set woman in a floral muumuu with black beehive hair and Cleopatra eye make-up hauling herself out of a chair as overstuffed as she was; twenty years ago she probably looked like Elizabeth Taylor. Now she looked more like John Belushi *doing* Elizabeth Taylor.

"Twenty-six dollars," she informed him, pushing the register his way. "Cash, check or credit card?"

"Cash."

She looked at him, for the first time, and her heavily mascaraed eyes froze.

"Jesus Christ," she said.

"What's wrong, lady?"

"Nuh . . . nothing."

He signed the register and she stood there gaping at him; she hadn't returned to her soap opera when he exited, standing there frozen, an obese Lot's wife.

In his room, he tossed his duffel bag on the bureau, turned on the TV to CNN, just for the noise, and sat on the bed by the nightstand. He found the slim Greenwood phone book in the top drawer, next to the Gideon Bible, and he thumbed through it, looking for an address. He wrote it down on the notepad by the phone.

It was getting close enough to suppertime that he couldn't go calling on people. But small-town people ate early, so by seven or maybe even six-thirty, he could risk it. He'd been raised in a small town himself, back in Indiana—not this small, but small enough.

He showered, shaved, and after he'd splashed cold water on his face, he studied it in the bathroom mirror as if looking for clues: gray-blue eyes, high cheekbones, narrow nose, dimpled chin. Then he shrugged at himself, and ran a hand through his long, shaggy, wheat-colored hair; that was all the more attention he ever paid to it.

Slipping back into his jeans, pulling on a light-blue polo shirt, he hoped he looked presentable enough not to get chased away when he showed up on a certain doorstep. He breathed deep, half sigh, half determination.

He'd not be turned away.

Greenwood wasn't big enough to rate a McDonald's, apparently, but there was a Dairy Freez and a Mr. Quik-Burger, whatever that was. He passed up both, walking along a shady, idyllic residential street, with homes dating mostly to the 1920s or before he'd guess, and well kept. Finally he came to the downtown, which seemed relatively prosperous: a corner supermarket, video store, numerous bars, and a cafe called Mom's.

Somebody somewhere had told him that one of the three rules of life was not eating at any restaurant called Mom's; one of the others was not playing cards with anybody named

Doc. He'd forgotten the third, and proved the first wrong by having the chicken fried steak, American fries with gravy, corn and slaw, and finding them delicious.

The only thing wrong with Mom's was that it was fairly busy—farm families, blue-collar folks—all of whom kept looking at him. It was as if he was wearing a "Kick Me" sign, only they weren't smirking: they had wide, hollow eyes, and whispered. Husbands and wives would put their heads together, mothers would place lips near a child's ear for a hushed explanation.

Jeff's dad, back in Indiana, was not much of a man's man; Dad was a drama teacher at a small college, and if it hadn't been for Uncle Fred, Jeff would never have learned to hunt and fish and shoot. But Jeff's dad's "guilty pleasure" (Dad's term) was John Wayne movies, and other westerns. Jeff loved them, too. "The Searchers" he had seen maybe a million times—wore out the videotape.

But right now he felt like Randolph Scott or maybe Audie Murphy in one of those '50s westerns where a stranger came to town and everybody looked at him funny.

Or maybe it was just his imagination: he was sitting in the corner of the cafe, and to his left, up on the wall, after all, was a little chalkboard with the specials of the day.

His waitress wasn't looking at him funny; she was a blonde of perhaps fifteen, pretty and plump, about to burst the buttons of her waitress uniform. She wanted to flirt, but Jeff wasn't in the mood.

When she brought the bill, however, he asked her directions to the address he'd written on the notepaper.

"That's just up the street to Main, and two blocks left and one more right," she said. "I could show you . . . I get off at eight."

"That's okay. How old are you?"

"Eighteen. That little pin you're wearing . . . were you really in Desert Storm?"

He had forgotten it was on there. "Uh, yeah."

"See any action?"

He nodded, digging some paper money out of his pocket. "Yeah, a little."

Her round pretty face beamed. "Greenwood's gonna seem awful dull, after that. My name's Tabitha, but my friends call me Tabby."

"Hi, Tabby."

"My folks just moved here, six months ago. Dad works at Chemco?"

"Mmmm," Jeff said, as if that meant something to him. He was leaving a five-dollar bill and an extra buck, which covered the food and a tip.

"Jenkins!" somebody called.

It was the manager, or at least the guy in the shirt and tie behind the register up front; he was about fifty with dark hair, a pot belly and an irritated expression.

"You got orders up!" he said, scowling over at the girl.

Then he saw Jeff and his red face whitened.

"What's with him?" Tabby asked under her breath. "Looks like he saw a ghost. . . ."

The pleasantly plump waitress swished away quickly and Jeff, face burning from all the eyes on him, got the hell out of there.

At dusk, in the cool breeze, Greenwood seemed unreal, like something Hollywood dreamed up; as he walked back into the residential neighborhood—earlier, he must have walked by within a block of the address he was seeking—he was thinking how perfect it seemed, when a red pick-up rolled by with speakers blasting a Metallica song.

He hated that shit. Heavy metal was not his style, or drugs, either. His folks liked to joke about being "old hippies," and indeed he'd grown up used to the smell of incense and the sweet sickening aroma of pot. They weren't potheads or anything, but now and then, on a weekend night at home, they'd go in the den and put on Hendrix or Cream (music Jeff didn't care for in the least) and talk about the good old days.

Jeff loved his parents, but that Woodstock crap made him sick. He liked country western music—Garth Brooks, Travis Tritt—and found his folks' liberal politics naive. Some of his views came from Uncle Fred, no question; and maybe, like most kids, Jeff was just inclined to be contrary to his parents.

But a part of him had always felt apart from them. A stranger.

If it hadn't been for Dad liking western movies (Mom hated them, and never had a kind word for "that fascist John Wayne"), they might not have bonded at all. But when his father was a kid, "Gunsmoke" and "Have Gun Will Travel" were on TV, and that bug had bit his dad before the Beatles came along to screw up Jeff's parents' entire generation.

The streetlamp out front was burned out, but a light was on over of the door of the one-and-a-half story 1950s era brick bungalow, with its four steps up to a stoop and its lighted doorbell. It was as if he were expected.

But he wasn't.

And he stood on the stoop the longest time before he finally had the nerve to push the bell.

The door opened all the way—not just a protective crack: this was still a small enough, safe enough town to warrant such confidence, or naivete. The cheerful looking woman standing there, in a yellow halter top and red shorts and yellow-and-red open-toed sandals, was slender and red-headed with pale freckled-all-over skin; she was green-eyed, pug-

110

nosed, with full lips—attractive but not beautiful, and probably about thirty.

"Danny," she began, obviously expecting somebody else, a bottle of Coors in a red-nailed hand, "I . . ."

Then her wide smile dissolved and her eyes widened and, saying "Jesus Christ!" she dropped the Coors; it exploded on the porch, and Jeff jumped back.

She was breathing hard, looking at him, ignoring the foaming beer and the broken glass between them.

"What . . . what is . . . who . . ."

Her eyes tightened and shifted, as if she were trying to get him in focus.

"Mrs. Hastings, I'm sorry to just drop in on you like this."

Her voice was breathless, disbelieving: "Carl?"

"My name is Jeff Carson, Mrs. Hastings. We spoke on the phone?"

"Step into the light. Mind the glass. . . ."

He did.

Her eyes widened again and her mouth was open; her full lips were quivering. "It's not possible."

"I called inquiring about your husband. And you told me he had died recently."

"Six months ago. I don't understand. . . ."

"Is there somewhere we could talk? You seem to be expecting somebody. . . ."

She nodded; swallowed. "Mr. Carson . . . Jeff?"

"Please."

"There's a deck in back; I was just relaxing there. Would you mind walking around, and meeting me there? I don't . . . don't want you walking through the house just yet. My son is playing Nintendo and I . . . don't want to disturb him."

That made as little sense as anything else, but Jeff merely nodded.

In back, up some steps onto the wooden sun deck, Jeff sat in a white metal patio chair by a white metal table under a colorful umbrella; dusk was darkening into evening, and the back yard stretched endlessly to a break of trees. A bug light snapped and popped, eating mosquitoes; but a few managed to nibble Jeff, just the same.

In a minute or so, she appeared through a glass door. She had two beers, this time; she handed him one, and took a man-like gulp from the other.

"So you're the one who called," she said.

"That's right."

"I almost forgot about that. All you did was ask for Carl, and when I said he'd died, you just said 'oh,' and asked when, and I said not long ago, and you said you were very sorry and hung up. Right? Wasn't that the conversation?"

"That was the conversation."

"Are you his son?"

That surprised Jeff, but he nodded and said, "How did you know? Is there . . . a resemblance?"

She had a mouthful of beer and almost spit it out. "Wait here."

She went inside the house and came back with a framed color photograph of a man in a sheriff's uniform and hat—gray-blue eyes, high cheekbones, narrow nose, dimpled chin. Jeff might have been looking into a mirror of the future, showing him what he would look like in twenty-one years.

"No wonder everybody's been looking at me weird," he said. He couldn't stop staring at the picture; his hand shook.

"You never met him?"

"No. Except for this afternoon."

"This afternoon?"

"At the cemetery."

And then Jeff began to cry.

Mrs. Hastings rose and came over and put her arm around him; patted his shoulder, as if to say, There there. "Listen . . . what's your name?"

"Jeff."

She moved away as Jeff dried his eyes with fingertips. "Jeff, I never knew about you. Carl never told me. We were married a long time, but he never said anything about you."

"He was the local sheriff?"

"Yes. City, not county. For twelve years. You don't know much about your dad, do you?"

"My dad . . . my dad is a man named Stephen Carson."

"I don't understand."

"I was adopted." He said the obvious: "Carl Hastings was my natural father."

She was sitting again. She said, "Oh," drawing it out into a very long word. Then she pointed at him. "And the mother was Margie Holdaway!"

"That's right. How did you know?"

"Carl and Margie were an item in high school. Oh, I was just in grade school at the time, myself, but I've heard all about it. Not from Carl . . . from the gossips in this town that wanted to make sure I knew all about the Boy Most Likely and his hot affair with the Homecoming Queen. I just never knew anything had . . . come of it."

"Tell me about him."

"You . . . you don't know anything about him, do you, Jeff?"

"No. I always wanted to know who my real parents were. My *folks* knew . . . they didn't get me from an agency. There was some connection between dad, that is, Stephen Carson, and a lawyer who went to school with Margie Holdaway's father. Anyway, that's how the adoption was arranged. My parents told me that when I turned twenty-one, if I still

113

wanted to know who my natural parents were, they'd tell me. And they did."

"And you came looking for your dad."

"Six months too late, it looks like. Tell me about him."

She told him. Carl Hastings was an only child, a farm boy from around Greenwood who was one of the little town's favorite sons—a high-school football star (All-State), he had gone on to a scholarship and a successful run of college ball that led to pro offers. But in his senior year, Carl had broken his leg in the final game of the season. He had returned to Greenwood, where he went to work for a car dealership.

"My *daddy's* business," Mrs. Hastings said, and she sipped her Coors. "I was ten years younger than Carl . . . your daddy. I was working in the Greenwood Pontiac Sales office, just out of high school, and things just sort of developed." She smiled and gazed upward, and inward; shook her head. "Carl was just about the handsomest man I ever saw. Least, till you came to my door."

"When did he become sheriff?"

She smirked a little, shook her head. "After we got married, Carl felt funny about working for his wife's daddy. Shouldn't have, but he did. When he got promoted to manager, he just . . . brooded. He was a funny sort of guy, your daddy . . . very moral. Lots of integrity. Too much, maybe."

"Why do you say that?"

"Oh, I don't know. It was his only fault, really. . . . He could be kind of a stuffed shirt. Couldn't roll with the flow, or cut people much slack."

"Did that make him a good sheriff or a bad one?"

"He was re-elected five times, if that answers your question. He was the most dedicated lawman you can imagine."

"Is that what got him killed?"

The words hit her like a physical blow. She swallowed; her

eyes began to go moist. She nodded. "I . . . I guess it was."

"I know it must be painful, ma'am. But what were the circumstances?"

Her expression froze, and then she smiled. "The way you said that . . . you said it, *phrased* it, just like Carl would have. Right down to the 'ma'am.' "

"How did my father die?"

"It *is* painful for me to talk about. If you wait a few minutes, Danny Simmons is stopping by. . . ."

As if on cue, a man in the uniform of the local sheriff, came out through the house, via the glass doors; he was not Carl Hastings, of course: he was a tall, dark-haired man with angular features, wearing his sunglasses even though darkness had fallen.

"I let myself in, babe—I think Tim's gone numb from Nintendo . . . Judas Priest!"

The man in the sheriff's uniform whipped off his sunglasses to get a better look; his exclamation of surprise was at seeing Jeff.

"Danny—this is Carl's son." She had stood and was gesturing to Jeff, who slowly rose himself.

"Jesus, Annie." Simmons looked like he'd been pole-axed. "I didn't know Carl had a son, except for Tim."

"Neither did I," she said.

"He was my natural father," Jeff said, extending his hand, and the two men shook in the midst of the explanation.

"Adopted, huh? I'll bet I know who the mother was," Simmons said, tactlessly, finding a metal patio chair to deposit his lanky frame in. "Margie Sterling."

"I thought her name was Holdaway," Jeff said.

"Maiden name," Mrs. Hastings explained. "Margie married Al Sterling right after college."

"Al Sterling?"

"His Honor Alfred Sterling," Simmons said, with a faint edge of nasty sarcasm. "Circuit judge. Of course, he wasn't a judge when Margie married him . . . he was just the golden boy who was supposed to take the legal profession by storm."

"And didn't?" Jeff asked.

Sheriff Simmons leaned forward and Jeff could smell liquor on the man's breath, perhaps explaining the obnoxious behavior. "Fell on his ass in New York City with some major firm. Came crawling back to Greenwood to work in his daddy's law office. Now he's the biggest tight-ass judge around. You got a beer for me, babe?"

A little disgusted, a little irritated, Mrs. Hastings said, "Sure you need it, Danny?"

"I'd have to go some, to match that lush Sterling." He turned to Jeff and shrugged and smiled. "Have to forgive me, kid. I had a long day."

"No problem. Did you work with my father?"

"Proud to say I did. I was his deputy for five, no six, years. Stepping into his shoes was the hardest, biggest thing I ever had to try to do."

"Mrs. Hastings suggested I ask you about how he died."

Simmons lost his confident, smirky expression; he seemed genuinely sorrowful when he said, "Sorry, kid—I thought you knew."

"No. That's why I'm here. I'm trying to find out about him."

Simmons seemed to be tasting something foul. "Punks . . . goddamn gang scum."

"Gangs? In a little town like this?"

"Oh, they're not local. They come in from the big cities, looking for farmhouses to rent and set up as crack houses, quiet rural areas where they can do their drug trafficking out

116

of and don't have big-city law enforcement to bother 'em.' "

"You've got that kind of thing going on here?"

Mrs. Hastings smiled proudly as she said, "Not now—Carl chased 'em out. He and Danny shot it out with a bad-ass bunch and chased 'em out of the county."

"No kidding," Jeff said. He felt a surge of pride. Had his real dad *been* John Wayne?

"That was about two weeks before it happened," Simmons said softly.

"Before what happened?"

Mrs. Hastings stood, abruptly, said, "I'm getting myself another beer. Anybody else?"

"No thanks," Jeff said.

"I already asked for one and didn't get it," Simmons reminded her.

She nodded and went inside.

Simmons leaned forward, hands folded, elbows on his knees. "It wasn't pretty. Classic urban-style drive-by shooting—as he come out of the office, some nameless faceless asshole let loose of a twelve-gauge shotgun and . . . sorry. Practically blew his head off."

Jeff winced. "Anybody see it?"

"Not a soul. It was three in the morning; we'd had a big accident out on the highway and he worked late. Office is downtown, and about then, it's deserted as hell. Practically tumbleweeds blowin' through."

"Then how do you know it was that gang retaliating?"

Simmons shrugged. "Just the M.O., really. And we did have a report that a van of those spic bastards was spotted rolling through town that afternoon."

"It was an Hispanic gang?"

"That's what I said."

"Nobody else had a motive?"

"You mean, to kill your dad? Kid, they would have elected that man president around here if they could. Everybody loved him."

"Not quite everybody," Jeff said.

Mrs. Hastings came back out and sat herself and her Coors back down. She still hadn't brought Simmons one.

"Sorry," she said. "I just didn't want to have to hear that again."

"I don't blame you," Jeff said. "I need to ask you something, and I don't mean for it to be embarrassing or anything."

"Go ahead," she said guardedly.

"Were my father and Margie Sterling still . . . friends?"

Her expression froze; then she sighed. Then she looked at the bottle of beer as her thumb traced a line in the moisture there. "You'll have to ask her that."

"You think she'd be around?"

"Probably. I can give you the address."

"I'd appreciate that."

Then she smiled, one-sidely, and it was kind of nasty. "Like to see the expression on her face when she gets a load of *you*. Excuse me a second—I'll go write that address down for you."

She got up and went inside again.

Simmons lounged his scarecrow-like body back in the patio chair and smiled affably. "So how long you going to be in town?"

"As long as it takes."

"To do what?"

"Find out why my father was killed."

The smile disappeared. "Look . . . kid. We investigated ourselves; plus, we had state investigators in. It was a gang shooting."

"Really? What gang exactly?"

"We didn't take their pedigree when Carl and me ran 'em off that farm!"

"You must have had a warrant."

"We did. It was a John Doe. Hey, hell with you, kid. You don't know me, and you don't know our town, and you didn't even know your damn father."

"Why do you call my father's wife 'babe'?"

"What?"

"You heard me."

Mrs. Hastings came back out with the address on a slip of paper. She handed it to Jeff.

"Good luck," she said, and then, suddenly, she touched his face. Her hand was cold and moist from the beer bottle she'd been holding, but the gesture was overwhelmingly warm. He looked deep into the moist green eyes and found only love for his late father.

"You can answer my question later," he said to the sheriff, and walked down the steps off and away from the deck.

The Sterling house was as close to a mansion as Greenwood had: on the outskirts of town, in a housing development of split-level homes that looked as expensive as they did similar, dominating a circular cul-de-sac, was a much larger structure, plantation-like, white, with pillars; through a large multi-paned octagonal window high above the entry, a chandelier glimmered.

He rang the bell and an endlessly bing-bonging theme played behind the massive mahogany door; a tall narrow row of windows on either side of the door provided a glimpse of a marble-floored entryway beyond.

He half expected a butler to answer, but instead it was a woman in a sweatshirt and slacks; at first he thought she was the housekeeper, but she wasn't.

She was his mother.

She was small and attractive—she had been cute, no doubt, when his father had dated her a lifetime ago; now she was a pixie-woman with short brown hair and wide-set eyes and a thin, pretty mouth. The only sign of wealth was a massive glittering diamond on the hand she brought up to her mouth, as she gasped at the sight of him.

". . . Carl?" Her voice was high-pitched, breathy, like a little girl's.

"No," Jeff said.

"You're not Carl. Who . . ."

Then she knew.

She didn't say so, but her eyes told him, *she knew,* and she stepped back and slammed the door in his face.

He stood staring at it for a while, and was just starting to get angry, finger poised to press the bell again, and again, for an hour, for forever if he had to, when the door opened, slowly, and she looked at him. She had gray-blue eyes, too. Maybe his eyes had come from her, not his father.

Then the little woman threw herself around him. Held him. She was weeping. Pretty soon he was weeping, too. They stood outside the mansion-like home and held each other, and comforted each other, until a male voice said, "What *is* this?"

They moved apart, turned to see a man who could have been forty or could have been fifty, but his dark eyes seemed dead already; a thin, gray-haired individual whose once-handsome features were tightened into a clenched fist of a face. He wore a button-down sweater over a pale blue shirt with a tie; the guy really knew how to relax in the evening. He had a pipe in one hand and a large cocktail glass in the other.

"What the hell is this about?" he demanded, but his voice was thin and whiny.

She pulled Jeff into the light. "Al—this is my son." Then she turned to Jeff and asked, "What's your name?"

Soon Jeff and Mrs. Sterling were seated on high chrome stools at the ceramic-tile island in the center of a large kitchen, with endless dark-wood cabinets, appliance-loaded countertops and stained-glass windows. She had served him chocolate chip cookies and tea; the pot was still simmering on one of the burners opposite them on the ceramic island.

Judge Sterling had, almost immediately, gotten out of their way, saying morosely, "You'll be wanting some privacy," and disappearing into a study.

"I told Al all about my youthful pregnancy," she said. "We're both Catholic and I like to think he respects my decision to have you."

"I'm certainly glad you did," he said, and smiled. This should have felt awkward, but it didn't. He felt he'd always known this pretty little woman.

"I didn't show at all," she said. "When we graduated, I was six months along and no one even guessed. I had you late that summer, and then started college a few weeks later . . . never missed a beat."

She had a perky way about her that endeared her to him immediately.

"I hope . . . I hope you can forgive me for never getting in touch with you. That's just the way it was done, in those days. I don't know how it is now, but when you gave up a baby back then, you gave him up. His new parents *were* his parents."

"I don't hold any grudge. Not at all. I had good parents. I had a fine childhood."

She touched his hand; stroked it, soothingly. "I hope so.

And I want to hear all about it. I hope we can be . . . friends, at least."

"I hope so, too."

He told her about his parents' pledge to reveal his true parentage to him, at his twenty-first birthday.

"My only regret . . . my only resentment toward my folks . . . is that, by making me wait, they cost me knowing . . . or even meeting . . . my real father."

She nodded, and her eyes were damp. "I know. That's a terrible thing. I know everyone's already told you, but you're a dead ringer for your dad . . . poor choice of words. I'm sorry."

"That's why I'm here, actually. The main reason."

"What do you mean?"

"To find out why and how my father died."

"Who have you spoken to?"

He filled her in.

"Terrible thing," she said, "what those gang kids did."

"You believe he died that way?"

"Oh, yes. We were proud of him, locally . . ." She lowered her voice. ". . . although the Board of Inquiry, into the farmhouse shooting, which my husband oversaw, was pretty hard on Carl and Dan."

"Really?"

"They were both suspended without pay for a month. Excessive use of force. Overstepping certain bonds of legal procedure . . . I don't know what, exactly. I'm afraid . . . nothing."

"What?"

She leaned close. "I'm afraid Alfred may have used the situation to get back at Carl."

"Your . . . romance with my father . . . it was strictly a high-school affair, wasn't it?"

She scooted off the chrome stool to get the teakettle and pour herself another cup. Her back was to him when she said, "It wasn't entirely a . . . high-school . . . affair."

He nibbled at a chocolate chip cookie; it was sweet and good. He wondered if it was homemade, and if so, if a cook had made it, or if his mother had.

She was seated again, stirring sugar into her tea. "For a lot of years, we didn't even speak, your father and I. Both our parents had made sure we were kept apart . . . we went to different colleges . . . the pregnancy—please don't take this wrong—but it was a tragedy in our lives, not the joy it should have been. The baby . . . you . . . broke us apart, instead of bringing us together, like it should." She shook her head. "Times were different."

"You don't have to apologize. I don't need explanations. I just want to know . . . the basic facts. The . . . truth."

"The truth is, your dad and I would see each other, around town . . . I moved back here, oh, ten years ago, when Al's New York law practice didn't work out . . . and when we passed at the grocery store or on the street, Carl and me, we'd smile kind of nervously, nod from a distance, never even speak, really."

"I understand. Kind of embarrassed about it."

"Right! Well . . . last year . . . no, it was a year and a half ago . . . Al and I were separated for a time. We have two children, both college-age, boy and a girl . . . they're your half-brother and sister, you know. You *do* have some catching up to do."

That was an understatement.

"Anyway, when the kids moved out, I moved out. It's . . . the details aren't important. Anyway, we were separated, and as fate would have it, Carl and Annie were having some problems, too. Carl and I, we ran into each other at one of the local bars one night, kind of started crying into each other's beer . . . and it just happened."

"You got romantic again."

She nodded; studied her tea, as if the leaves might tell her something about the future—or the past. "It was brief. Like I said, I'm Catholic and have certain beliefs, and Al and I decided to go to marriage counseling, and Carl and Annie got back together, and . . . that was the end of it."

"I see."

She touched his hand again; clutched it. "But it was a sweet two weeks, Jeff. It was a reminder of what could have been. Maybe, what should have been."

"I see. The trouble my father and his wife were having, did it have anything to do with his deputy?"

"That weasel Danny Simmons? How did *you* know?"

"He was over at her house tonight. Calling her 'babe.' "

She laughed humorlessly. "She and Danny did have an affair. Cheap fling is more like it. Danny *was* the problem between her and Carl. Your father . . . he was too straight an arrow to have ever run around on her—anyway, before she had run around on him."

"But they got back together?"

"They did. And just because Annie and Danny have drifted back together, don't take it wrong. I truly believe she loved your father, and that they'd found their way back to each other."

"Well, she's found her way back to Simmons, now."

"You shouldn't blame her. People make wrong choices sometimes . . . particularly when they're at a low ebb, emotionally."

"Well . . . I suppose she can use a man in her life, with a son to raise. Was there any sort of pension from my father being sheriff, or some kind of insurance? I mean, he was shot in the line of duty."

"I'm sure there is. But don't worry about Annie Hastings, financially. Her father's car dealership is one of the most successful businesses in the county, and she's an only child."

He slid off the stool. "Well . . . thank you, Mrs. Sterling. You've been very gracious."

"Must you go?"

"I think I should." He grinned at her. "The cookies were great. Did you make them?"

"I sure did." She climbed off her stool and came up and hugged him. "Any time you want some more, you just holler. We're going to get to know each other, Jeff. And Jeff?"

"Yes?"

"Would you work on something for me?"

"What's that?"

"See if you can work yourself up to calling me 'mom'—instead of Mrs. Sterling."

"Okay," he said.

She saw him to the door. Before he left, she tugged on his arm, pulling him sideways, and pecked his cheek. "You be good."

He started to say something, but then noticed her face was streaked with tears and suddenly he couldn't talk. He nodded and walked away.

It was approaching ten o'clock now, and he walked back downtown; he wanted to see where his father worked, and around the corner from Mom's Cafe (now closed), he found the County Sheriff's office, a one story tan-brick building. He stood staring at the sidewalk out front, heavily bathed in light from a nearby streetlamp. He knelt, touched the cement, wondering where his father's blood had been. Heavy bushes were to the right and left of the sidewalk and Jeff squinted at them. Then he looked up at the streetlamp and squinted again.

125

★ ★ ★ ★ ★

The sheriff's brown and white vehicle was still parked in front of the Hastings home. Jeff leaned against the car, waiting, hoping Simmons wouldn't be spending the night.

At a little after eleven, the tall sheriff came loping around from behind the house—apparently, they'd stayed out on the deck this whole time.

"Who is that?"

"Can't you see me?"

He chuckled, hung his thumbs in his leather gun belt. "The Hastings kid. No, I couldn't see you—streetlight's out."

"Actually, my name is Carson. The streetlight wasn't out in front of my father's office, was it?"

Simmons frowned; his angular face was a shadowy mask in the night. "What are you talking about?"

"Annie Hastings stands to come into her share of money, one of these days, doesn't she? Her father owns that car dealership and all."

"Yeah. So?"

"So I figure she wasn't in on it."

"On what?"

"Murdering my father."

Silence hung like a curtain. Crickets called; somewhere tires squealed.

"Your father was killed by street-gang trash."

"He was killed by trash, all right. But it wasn't a street gang. Out in front of the sheriff's office, my father couldn't have been cut down in a drive-by shooting; he'd have dived for the bushes, or back inside. He'd have got a shot off in his own defense, at least."

"That's just nonsense."

"I think it was somebody who knew him. Somebody who

called to him, who he turned to, who shot his head off. I think it was you. You wanted his job, and you wanted his wife."

"You're just talking."

"All I want to know is, was she in on it?"

Simmons didn't answer; he went around the car, to the driver's side door.

Jeff followed, grabbed the man's wrist as he reached for the car-door handle. "Was his wife in on it? Tell me!"

Simmons shoved him away. "Go away. Go home! Go back to Iowa or wherever the hell."

"Indiana."

"Wherever the hell! Go home!"

"No. I'm staying right here in Greenwood. Asking questions. Poking my nose in. Looking at the files, the autopsy, the crime-scene report, talking to the state cops, putting it all together until you're inside a cell where you belong."

Simmons smiled. It seemed friendly. "This is just a misunderstanding," he said, and slipped his arm around Jeff's shoulder, all chummy, when the gun was out of its holster and in Jeff's midsection now.

"Let's take a walk," Simmons said, softly; the arm around Jeff's shoulder had slipped around his neck and turned into a near chokehold. "There's some trees behind the house. We'll . . ."

Jeff flipped the man and the sheriff landed hard on the pavement, on his back, but dazed or not, Simmons brought the gun up, his face a thin satanic grimace, and fired, exploding the night.

The car window on the driver's side spider-webbed as Jeff ducked out of the way, and with a swift martial art kick, he sent the gun flying out of Simmons' hand and it sailed and fell, nearby, with a *thunk*. The sheriff was getting to his feet but another almost invisible kick put him back down again, unconscious.

The night was quiet. Crickets. An automobile, somewhere. Despite the shot, no porch lights were popping on.

Jeff walked over to where the gun had landed. He picked it up, enjoyed the cool steel feel of the revolver in his hand, walked back to the unconscious Simmons, cocked it, pointed it down, and studied the skinny son of a bitch who had killed his father.

"It's not what your father would have done," she said.

He turned and Annie Hastings was standing there. At first he thought she had a gun in her hand, but it was only another Coors.

He said, "Did you hear any of that?"

She nodded. "Enough."

"He killed your husband."

"I believe he did."

"You didn't know?"

"I didn't know."

"You weren't part of it?"

"No, I wasn't."

"Can I trust you?"

"You'll know as much," she said, swigging the beer, then smiling bitterly, "when I back you up in court."

He stood at the gravestone in the cemetery on the hillside. He studied the words: *Carl Henry Hastings—Beloved Husband, Loving Father. 1954-1992.* He touched the carved letters: *Father.* He said a silent prayer.

The wind whispered a response, through the trees.

"What was he like?" he asked. "What was he *really* like?"

His mother smiled; her pretty pixie face made him happy.

"He was like you," she said. "He was just like you."

FOURTH OF JULY

Firecracker Kill

Summer in the City, hot and gritty, like the song said, the Fourth of July fast approaching; countless windows, walls and telephone poles, from Greek Town to New Harlem, were plastered with posters and handbills advertising the upcoming Independence Day Festival.

The festival was a nighttime affair, which was good, because the nights were cooler. Right now the days hung heavy with a humid heat that made walking down the street a stroll through a blast furnace.

And police detective Stan Rasher was running.

Running down an alley after the son of a bitch who, as informants had indicated, was hanging around Westburg Elementary offering little girls rides home—lap rides. Rasher—twenty-eight, slim, dark, as snappy a dresser as his pay would allow—hadn't even shown the guy his badge yet, was just approaching him coolly and casually and conversationally, but the pervert had finely honed instincts, and made Rasher as a cop and threw the detective against the chain wire of the schoolyard fence. Now, four blocks later, in the rundown business district of the old downtown, Rasher was right behind the bastard, who was running toward another chain link fence at the alley's end.

Only this time it was the pervert who got thrown against the fence, bouncing off it into some nearby garbage cans,

129

causing a clatter, sending a stray cat screeching and scurrying.

"Don't hurt me!" the guy was saying, in near tears. He
looked harmless—about twenty-two, clean-shaven, neatly
dressed, his persona reeking trustworthiness; he might be
Uncle Bob, or even Daddy. But he wasn't. He was human
garbage, right at home sprawled amid those trash cans.

A few minutes later, Rasher was turning the perp over to
Lt. Price from the 32nd Precinct.

"I thought you were working Homicide," Price said,
shoving Rasher's prisoner into the back of a black-and-white.
Like Rasher, Price came from a long line of cops—including
Price's brother, the chief. The husky ex-Infantry sergeant had
a reputation for the rough and tumble.

"Yeah, well they got me on loan-out to Vice," Rasher said,
trying to smooth out his suit coat. He was soaked with sweat.

"Not pretty duty," Price said.

"I hate it," Rasher said cheerfully.

And he did.

Price shook his head. "The worst is these young girls, kids,
runaways, caught up in this slimy scene."

The perp was looking blankly out the rear window at them
and Price rapped the window, and the guy reared back as if
the blow had hit him.

"Enough to make you ashamed to be packing a pistol,"
Price said.

"Men are the worst," Rasher agreed.

A crowd had gathered, a mixture that included merchants,
some white-collar workers and a sprinkling of homeless. Lost
among them was a seemingly innocuous figure of average
height, pudgy not fat, balding not bald, a man of around forty
in red bow tie, sweat-circled white shirt and baggy navy blue
pants, wire frame glasses riding the pug nose of a strangely

child-like face. He watched with bland interest, apparently in no hurry to get anywhere.

Finally, the observer strolled down the block and stepped into the reception area of his nearby storefront business, announced on the window as ROSE PHOTOGRAPHY, locking the door, the CLOSED sign turned out, and headed back to his studio, where a beautiful teenaged girl, arcs of brunette hair brushing her bare shoulders, sat nude, tied to a kitchen chair, a slash of duct tape over her mouth, her eyes wide with fear. Her tube top, cut-off jeans and panties were torn discarded fragments scattered about the room.

"Nothing to worry about," he said. "That commotion outside doesn't concern us. . . ."

And he began taking photos of the woman, telling her to "Smile," despite the duct tape.

The next morning just before eleven, at Central City Headquarters, Rasher—whose beeper had summoned him— arrived at the desk of the commander of the detective division, Inspector Dan Fitch.

Fitch, his flesh nearly as gray as his hair, his face almost as rumpled as his suit, handed Rasher a photo in a poly evidence bag.

Rasher found himself looking at a close-up of an attractive girl of perhaps sixteen; it was difficult to know just how attractive she was, because her features were distorted by the fat unlighted firecracker that had been stuffed in her mouth, like a sick phallic joke.

Her eyes were wide with terror.

"What's this?" Rasher asked.

"It came with these," Fitch said wearily, and handed him a half dozen more bagged photos of the girl, nude, duct-taped-tied to a chair.

"God, I hate Vice," Rasher sighed, pulling up a chair.

"You figure this girl's under age, right? We're talking child porn—"

"No. I'm taking you off Vice. This is Homicide."

"Murder?"

"Those photos came in the morning mail. These photos a police photographer took, last night, on the banks of Long River, near John Henry Tunnel."

A wave of sickness coursed through Rasher as he looked at the photos of the girl, the same girl, fat firecracker in her mouth, asprawl on the grass, hands duct-tape bound behind her, ankles—dead, now.

"This has all the earmarks of a serial killing," Fitch said. "But one corpse—however kinky—does not a serial killer make."

"Raped?" Rasher asked.

"No," Fitch said. "But there was semen in a Kleenex found near the body."

"Well, that gives us a blood type, at least."

"It's your case if you want it," Fitch said. "With your Homicide background, and your recent stint on Vice, you're the ideal man for the job."

"Dirty job."

"Which somebody has to do." Fitch shrugged. "Gets you off Vice."

"I'd pay the department for a shot at nailing this son of a bitch."

A smile joined the creases of Fitch's face. "You know, I can hear your father saying that."

In his six years on the department, Rasher had waited to hear Fitch say something akin to that; Fitch had been Rasher's father's best friend and, at the time of Pop's in-the-line-of-duty death, his partner. It had been Fitch who encouraged both Stan and his sister Melissa, who worked in

Records and Identification in this very building, to "join the family business."

This casual validation should have sent Rasher's spirits soaring; but that was impossible, with those grotesque photos spread out on the desk before him.

"You want me to partner up?" Rasher asked.

"You already are," Fitch said. "Now, don't start growling, but this is going to be an inter-agency operation."

"Shit—not the FBI—"

"Yes, the FBI. The Feds are disturbed over the serial killer-like aspects of this killing, and they're sending in a B.S.U. agent to work with you."

The Behavioral Science Unit—the Hannibal Lector squad.

"I have orders that go all the way up to Chief Price," Fitch said. "We're to keep a lid on this thing. We don't want to panic the public needlessly. . . ."

Rasher nodded.

"You'll report directly to me," Fitch said. "The FBI involvement in this case is not to be public—or even departmental—knowledge. Anybody asks, Agent Vint is in town doing statistical research on our improved crime rate."

Violent crime was down in the City. Tell that to this dead girl. . . .

"If anybody asks," Fitch continued, "you're merely Vint's p.d. liaison."

"You mean, I'm not even officially investigating this murder. . . ."

"No. Homicide already has a team on it, looking into the girl herself, her family, friends, the usual. The 'official' investigators won't even know you're exploring the serial-killer aspects of the case."

"This seems a little odd, Dan—"

"I'm counting on you, Stan. On your discretion."

Rasher shrugged. "Sure. Why not? Beats Vice. So what dark doorway do I meet my new partner in?"

"Meet him for an early lunch at Papa's."

"You're kidding . . ."

Fitch tapped one of the photos of the dead girl. "You think I'm in a mood to kid?"

Papa's Ristorante, a quaint hole-in-the-wall in Little Italy, was a legendary local fixture. Much the same could be said for the restaurant's owner, Angelo "Papa" Capuzzi. The Capuzzi family, whose fortune had been forged in booze, gambling and prostitution in the twenties, thirties and forties, claimed to be strictly legitimate, now. The Organized Crime task force, however, considered white-haired, genial Papa the reigning hereditary and administrative head of a crime family still very much enmeshed in illegal activities, save narcotics, which Papa reputedly forbade.

The maitre 'd led Rasher to Mr. Vint's booth, where Vint sat meticulously eating a plate of pasta. The FBI man wore a conservative but tailored gray suit, and his every graying hair was in place—late forties or early fifties, Rasher made him, though for a guy that age, Vint's face was oddly smooth, uncreased, as if it hadn't been used much, for smiling or frowning. His manner verged on prissiness; not a speck of red tomato sauce would get on this guy's shirt or suit coat, and he'd eaten half a loaf of bread without getting a crumb on the red-and-white checkered tablecloth.

After a handshake and brief introduction, Rasher cut to the chase. "So—what's prompted the FBI to get involved in a lone murder case, in such a hurry? The corpse is still warm."

Vint speared some linguini and twirled his fork. "Ever hear of Taurus?"

"The bull?"

Vint twitched a smile; his gray eyes were calm and cold. "The maniac."

Rasher lowered the menu he was examining. "You mean that freak in California, twenty years ago or so, who was giving Son of Sam a run for his money?"

"Right. Know much about him?"

"I know they never caught the bastard," Rasher said with a shrug. "I know they estimate he killed at least twenty young women. He left them nude, bound, no sexual molestation, but he masturbated near the corpses. An arrogant asshole, who taunted the cops . . ."

But Rasher found himself trailing off as his own words began registering on him in a shock of recognition: their potential serial killer indeed did resemble the Taurus killer, in style and flavor if not exact M.O. No wonder Fitch was worried about panicking the public. . . .

A waitress came over and Rasher ordered the cheese ravioli. Then he turned back to the impassive Vint.

"He wrote screwy letters to the press, didn't he?" Rasher asked. "Detailing his visions? Wasn't there some really crazed reason why he always killed young women. . . ."

"Taurus believes that those he kills in this life," Vint said, "will be his slaves in the next."

"So, naturally, he kills beautiful young babes," Rasher said wryly. "The Bob Guccione of serial killers."

"You've been working Vice, I understand. Taurus' victims, like that girl near the culvert last night, indicate our man is into bondage. Any ideas?"

"I know a few likely rocks to turn over."

After lunch, the two detectives drove to Irish Town and entered Pleasure World, one of the biggest XXX-shops in town; males, white- and blue-collar alike, studied the plastic-bagged magazines along the side walls; a rear wall displayed videotapes. Behind a display case of "sexual aides" (including whips and chains) slumped Merle, a heavy-set hood-eyed hardcase with Nixon-shadowed jowls and a stub of a cigar rolling in thick lips. Sitting on a stool, a wall of dildos behind him, his heavy arms folded, Merle wore a black Pleasure World T-shirt beneath which he seemed to be smuggling a Volkswagen beetle.

Vint whispered, "Doesn't look like the cooperative type."

"Merle's pretty tough," Rasher allowed. "But let's reason with him."

Merle's eyes were bored as Rasher requested a list of the porn merchants' clients who were heavily into bondage photos, particularly any clients who were into taking such photos themselves. And Rasher wanted to know who, locally, might provide models to a private individual interested in private bondage photo shoots, and the names of local photographers who might provide their services for bondage shoots.

"I gotta protect my clients' confidentiality," Merle said in a voice that seemed to ooze.

"You're not a lawyer," Rasher reminded him, "and you aren't a doctor."

"No," Merle said, and the cigar shifted as the thick lips smiled, "but my patrons trust me. And if we don't got trust in this world, what do we got?"

Rasher leaned against the glass counter. "Hear about that guy I busted yesterday? At the grade school?"

Merle shrugged.

"He had a shitload of kiddie porn in his apartment. Says he bought it here."

"That's a freakin' lie!" Merle said, rising off his stool.

"Well, I admit I don't think it's strong enough to go to the

D.A. with. Say, you know where we had lunch today?"

"I don't give a shit."

"Papa's—over in Little Italy. Some people say you work for the Capuzzis. Funny people, those Capuzzis. Selective about the sin they sell. Drugs for example, Papa won't go near that I hear. Wonder how he'd feel if somebody told him you were sellin' kiddie porn out the back door?"

"That's a damn lie."

"Yeah, well, Merle, you tell that to Papa's people, when they come around."

"You're an asshole, Rasher."

"Maybe." Rasher glanced around the shop at the garish obscene magazine and video covers. "I'd guess that's just one of the body parts you're an expert on."

Merle sneered; it was like a bad Elvis impression. "Come back in an hour and I'll have a list for you."

They did, and Merle did, and the rest of the day Rasher and Vint spent thinning the list out, deciding who to interview.

Down in Records and Identification, Rasher introduced Vint to Melissa, who was running several computer checks for them.

"You're pretty," Vint said.

"Why so surprised?" Melissa said, leaning across the counter. Her gold-highlighted brown curls brushed the shoulders of her white blouse; she was a shapely, green-eyed woman with a ready smile.

"You're *his* sister," Vint said, deadpan.

"Hey," Rasher said, "I'm not the worst lookin' guy on the planet."

"But you're not pretty," Vint said.

"You got me there. How long on those checks, Sis?"

"Five minutes."

"I'm getting back to my phone," Rasher said. "I got perverts to call . . . don't want to keep 'em hanging—some of 'em are upstanding citizens."

"Everybody needs a hobby," Vint said. "I'll wait."

And Rasher left Vint there with Melissa, who was finding her yen for older guys kicking in with this smooth-faced FBI man.

"You boys gonna knock off at a reasonable hour?" she asked him.

"Actually, we're going to stay at it."

"Double shift?"

Vint nodded. "Maniacs don't take much time off. They're sort of over-achievers."

"Oh."

"Why do you ask?"

She shrugged. "I get off at six. Thought maybe you'd like to have a drink."

Vint's smile was small but it was enormously winning, to Melissa, anyway. "America's a great country."

"Why's that?"

"Women asking men out."

"I wasn't asking you out. We're colleagues. Just thought you might like—"

"A drink? Sure."

They met at a little bar on a side street not far from head-quarters, a police hangout, and Melissa had expected her brother to be along, but when Vint came over and settled himself across from her in the booth, he was alone.

"I thought you and Stan were going to stay at it—"

"We are," he said. "But we divided up a few names. We can cover more ground working solo."

"Ah. Jeez, I guess I kind of screwed up."

"How's that?"

"I was counting on Stan for a ride over to the country club. See, I'm involved with the Miss Independence Day pageant, comin' up."

"Contestant?"

"No." She smiled, flattered. "I'm a little old for that."

"What are you, twenty-five?"

She was thirty-one. Twice divorced, childless, and thirty-one, damn it.

"Twenty-eight," she said.

"Hard to believe," he said.

"I am a former Miss Independence Day winner myself—never mind what year. I'm official chaperone for one of the girls."

"I'd be glad to give you a ride."

"Okay. Let's enjoy our drink and I'll take you up on that. . . ."

When he walked her to his parked silver Porsche, she was suitably impressed.

"Pretty snappy wheels for a cop," she said.

"I don't have a family to sap my income," he said.

He drove her to her pageant meeting at Eastwood Country Club; they parked in the shadow of the Starview Observatory, a domed structure on the edge of the country club golf course. The car windows were down, a blessedly cool breeze whispering in, respite from another hot humid day.

"You're nice," she said.

He looked handsome in the moonlight, and very young, despite the gray hair.

"No, I'm not," he said.

And he kissed her.

A tender little kiss that got hot suddenly, and Melissa pulled away, laughing, saying, "Thanks for the ride," and she slipped out of the car, into the night.

Vint watched her go, waited till he'd seen her enter the side door of the country club's stucco clubhouse, then drove to Highball's, a bar/disco on the edge of the warehouse district. The joint was run by a lounge lizard named Vernon Venall; Rasher's pal Merle had listed Venall as a likely provider of models for would-be bondage photographers.

Vint hadn't mentioned to Rasher that he knew Venall already.

Vint settled in at the bar and the proprietor sidled up and took the stool next to him. Venall wore in a sharkskin suit and skinny tie, apparel that hadn't been in style in the memory of any of the glittery-topped slit-skirted B-girls scattered around the joint. Forty-five, his short hair dyed an obvious black, his narrow blade of a pockmarked face distinguished by black little eyes as dead as a doll's, Venall said in his lacquered voice, "Buy you a drink, Vint?"

"Long as I don't have to drink it *with* you, Vernon."

"That's unkind."

"Read the paper today, Vernon?"

"I don't keep up with the news. Depresses me. World's gone to hell in a hand basket, you ask me."

"I was thinking more along the line of local news."

"If you're thinkin' what I think you're thinkin'. . . ."

"Some artwork doesn't need a signature for its artist to be obvious."

Venall swallowed, and it wasn't any of his drink. "I don't think it's him."

"Bull."

The double meaning of that made Vernon wince. "I can't tell you where he is without Mr. Roselli's say-so."

Vint sipped his Scotch. Nodded.

"Anything else?" Venall asked. "We through?"

"For now," Vint said.

And Vint quietly sat and finished his drink, and thought private thoughts. Just as he was about to leave, he noticed a slim young blonde in a blue spangly top and matching Spandex who was being hit on by two burly guys in business suits.

Not "hit on" in the usual bar sense: *hit* on. Slapping and shoving her around, and nobody was doing a damn thing about it—including Venall himself, who was pacing off to one side, adjusting his tie like Rodney Dangerfield.

Vint sighed and went over and tapped the nearest of the two guys on the shoulder. When the guy turned snarlingly toward him, Vint smiled blandly, saying, "Don't," waving a finger as though scolding a child.

Then Vint opened his coat and revealed the silenced nine-millimeter in the speed rig under his shoulder.

The two men backed off, patting the air, smiling nervously, and the blonde, in tears, clutched Vint's arm.

"Thank you, mister," she said. "They thought I was holding out on them. I wasn't, I swear to God I wasn't!"

"I believe you."

"Can I buy you a drink? Is there any way I can make it up to you?"

"No. I had selfish motives."

Her big blue eyes fluttered. "What?"

"I hate noise."

Shortly, when Vint approached his Porsche in the parking lot, a vice-like hand gripped him by either arm, from behind. One of the burly boys from inside was standing in front of Vint, grinning as he yanked the automatic from the shoulder rig, sticking it in his waistband. The guy had a bucket head, a lump of a nose and lamb-dropping eyes; he flashed Vint a badge.

"You shouldn't obstruct officers of the law," he said.

"In the line of duty," the one holding him said in Vint's ear.

Then Vint was hurled to the pavement, and they were standing over him, nightsticks in hand, poised to work him over.

Vint kicked the nearest one—the one who'd been holding him, a blond round-faced dope—in the groin, sprang to his feet like an acrobat and flipped the bucket-headed bastard to the pavement, where the guy did a belly flop in the empty pool of the parking lot. Both men were whimpering, but their suffering had just begun.

Vint turned the belly flopper over and retrieved his weapon from the guy's waistband, then kicked the nightstick from his hand, sending it clattering under a parked Buick. Then Vint plucked the other nightstick from the pavement, where the guy who had rolled himself in a groaning ball, clutching his groin, had dropped it.

And Vint used the nightstick on the pair, beating them senseless, breaking at least a few bones, their cries echoing in the warm but breezy night.

They were barely conscious as Vint tossed the nightstick like a spent cigarette, straightened his tie, said, "Didn't you hear me? I said 'Don't'," got into his Porsche and roared off.

The next morning of a brand-new sweltering day, Rasher was waiting at the counter of a cop hang-out coffee shop near headquarters, as they had prearranged.

Rasher, sipping coffee, felt a tap on his shoulder; he turned, but it wasn't Vint.

Cornelison, a lanky, seasoned detective he'd been working Vice with, leaned in, tickled about something. "Hear about Bates and Peterson?"

"No. Tell me it's good news, like a bus made roadkill out of 'em or something."

Bates and Peterson were two bent Vice cops that every moderately honest copper in Vice wished only the worst.

Cornelison chuckled. "Scuttlebutt is they were putting the arm on some hooker, at Highball's, when they made the mistake of going tangle-ass with that FBI guy you're running with."

"No shit?"

"None. They're both in the hospital. They got their clocks cleaned—worked over with their own nightsticks."

Cornelison chuckled again, patted Rasher on the back and moved on. Just as Vint came in out of the heat, wearing a perfect tan suit and looking like he'd never sweat a drop in his life, Rasher's beeper went off.

The homicide scene was a rural ditch northwest of town, in the back country. Fitch was there with a mobile crime unit, the whole nine yards. As Rasher and Vint approached, the older cop nodded, and jerked a thumb toward the ditch.

"I think we officially got ourselves a serial killer, boys," he said. "And he left his business card."

Rasher didn't get it. "What?"

Fitch held up an evidence bag with a crumpled Kleenex in it; another semen deposit.

She was brunette, probably fifteen, maybe sixteen, kind of plump, almost pretty, wrists duct-taped, ankles duct-taped, with a fat phallic firecracker stuffed in her mouth.

"Jesus," Rasher said, and he dropped to one knee, as if he were about to get knighted; instead, he lost his breakfast.

Doing this kept him too busy to notice Vint wandering the periphery, using a pencil to pick up a small empty Kodak .35 mm box, wordlessly pocketing it.

Later, in the Porsche, as they headed back to the City, Rasher said, "Sorry about back there."

"What?"

"Not very professional."

"What are you talking about?"

"Puking. I mean, I worked Homicide all last year. I saw worse things than that."

"It's the heat."

And the heat must have gotten even to Vint, because Rasher noticed the FBI agent's coat was unbuttoned, allowing a peek at the weapon in the fancy rig under his shoulder.

"Is that a silencer?"

Vint seemed embarrassed; with one hand, he buttoned his coat, as if he'd been caught with his fly down. "Yeah."

"Since when is a noise suppresser government issue?"

"Since never," Vint admitted. "What can I say? I hate noise."

Rasher was on the phone arranging interviews with perverts when Vint went down to Records and Identification, where Melissa came to the counter to greet him with a smile.

"How was rehearsal?" he asked her.

"Swell. Does my ego a lot of good, hanging around with a couple dozen beautiful eighteen and nineteen year-old goddesses."

"They're kids. You're a woman."

That made her beam. "I have a reception tonight, for the contestants. But it'll be over by ten—"

"First things first," Vint said. "I need you to run a fingerprint check for me."

He handed her a strip of tape with a print he had lifted from the Kodak box.

"Sure," she said. "But since you're not officially department, I need one of those inter-agency forms, you know—the 714JW?"

"I don't have it," he said, gesturing with open hands. "I

wasn't anticipating doing any investigating . . . this was supposed to be strictly statistical research. . . ."

She made a *click* in her cheek. "Yeah, and I can't call over and get one FAXed, either—FAXes aren't acceptable, by policy."

"I guess I can run over to the Bureau office, in Westburg . . ."

"Hell," she said, "give it here—you can lay the paperwork on me, later."

"Thanks," Vint said.

Rasher and Vint spent the rest of the morning on three interviews with convicted sex-crimes offenders, one an out-of-work school teacher in Greek Town, another a broker in the financial district off Axis Avenue, another a mechanic in El Barrio, where they were at an outdoor stand having tacos with sauce as hot as the day, when Rasher's beeper alerted them to a call for Vint from Melissa.

"You two sure are hitting it off," Rasher said with a grin.

"I won't get too friendly," Vint said. "I hear her brother packs heat."

Vint found his way to a pay phone.

"I have a name for you," Melissa said. "Michael Rose. Mean anything?"

"No," Vint lied.

"No criminal record, just military service. But here's an interesting wrinkle."

"He was discharged on a Section 8."

"How did you know?"

"Lucky guess."

". . . Maybe I'll see you later?"

"Yes, thanks," he said, more curtly than he meant, hanging up, too distracted to think of romance.

He sat back down at the picnic-style bench by the taco stand, next to Rasher.

"I checked in with my superior," Vint said. "We're going to have to split up this afternoon. Something from another case came up."

"No problem," Rasher said.

"Why don't we reconnoiter at Papa's around five?"

"Done."

That afternoon, alone, Vint entered the Rose Photography Studio in the old business district in Westburg. In the reception area, a beaming, pretty teenage girl was greeting her mother. Vint quickly got the drift that the girl had just had her photo taken for the Miss Independence Day pageant at the Fourth of July festival.

After mother and daughter exited, Vint turned the CLOSED sign around in the door, withdrew his noise-suppressed nine-millimeter and hit the little bell marked "Ring for Service."

And the pudgy, balding, baby-faced photographer himself came out to greet his newest customer, smiling. His smile faded when he saw the gun in Vint's hand, but then it almost immediately brightened again.

The photographer sat on a swivel seat at the customer counter and said to Vint, with a nervous chuckle, "Well . . . it's been a long time."

"Don't," Vint said, scolding him with a wagging finger.

"What do you mean, Vint?"

"You've started again. Stop."

The baby-faced photographer pushed his wire frames up on his pug nose. Mild indignation colored his tone as he said: "I'm sure I don't know *what* you're referring to."

Vint gestured with the long-snouted silenced automatic, like a teacher with a pointer. "This is a courtesy call . . . courtesy to your father, not to you. I'd rather kill you than look at you."

A pudgy hand splayed against a pudgy chest. "I've been good, I *have* been good . . ."

"End it or die. Those are your options. And that, Taurus, is no bull."

Vint tapped the air with the long-nosed gun.

"Don't," he repeated.

Then Vint turned the sign around so that OPEN faced the street, and he left.

At headquarters, Rasher was picking up some computer checks from his sister at Records and Identification when she casually dropped a bombshell.

"Remind Vint, will you," she said, "about getting me that inter-agency form, on that fingerprint?"

"What fingerprint?"

Soon Rasher was at his phone, calling over to the FBI office in Westburg, asking for Agent Vint. He went through several desks trying, but kept coming up empty.

"I'm sorry, Detective Rasher, no agent of that name works out of this office," said a division head, who was pretty high up the Bureau food chain. "And I don't come up with any agent of that name, at all, in the data base. . . ."

Rasher stood before Fitch's desk ticking off the items.

"He drives a Porsche, he packs a silenced weapon, he ran a fingerprint check without telling me, he worked a couple crooked cops over with a nightstick, an activity I might approve of but which seems a tad out of character for the FBI, who incidentally have never the hell heard of an agent Vint. . . ."

Fitch, looking weary, held up a hand. "You were to report strictly to me on this."

"What do you think I'm doin' right now?"

"You were told this was a covert operation, no one in the department was to know the true nature of your—"

"What the hell are you saying?"

Fitch's expression was pained. "A word to the wise, detective—investigate these killings, not your partner." The inspector tossed an evidence-bagged photo across the desk at Rasher. "That came in the morning mail."

The girl who'd been dead in the ditch was alive in the photo—but with a fat firecracker stuffed in the mouth of her terrified face.

"You know I want the son of a bitch doing this," Rasher said. "But how can you expect me to work with a partner I can't trust?"

"You want off the case, Stan? You want back on Vice?"

Rasher flipped the bagged photo back onto the desk. "You wouldn't pull this crap on my old man."

"You want off the case?"

"No, I don't want off the goddamn case!"

Just after five, at Papa's Ristorante, Rasher slid into the booth next to Vint, who was meticulously working on a plate of veal parmigiana. Slipping his hand beneath the table, Rasher cocked his revolver. The click was tiny, and tremendous.

The normally unresponsive Vint flinched.

"Thought you might recognize that sound," Rasher said. "The next sound will be louder, but just as familiar—and I know how you hate noise. . . ."

"What do you want, Stan?"

"I want you to spill your guts, or I'll spill 'em for you—right onto your napkin. Like some veal that slid off your plate. Talk to me, Vint—*now*."

A hand settled on Rasher's shoulder and he glanced up to see the gently smiling face of Papa Capuzzi. "You know, Stanley, your father never pulled a gun on a brother officer."

Papa pulled up a chair and sat across from them.

Astonished, Rasher watched the kindly looking man in the unassuming black suit and black tie as he began to speak, softly, slowly but surely, gesturing with both hands, like he was sculpting the air.

"There are those," Papa said, "who call me the local 'godfather'—what a silly thing, a Hollywood thing. I own a restaurant, Stanley, but I suppose I do have a certain . . . standing. A respect. Most people would respect me enough not pull a weapon, even under a table."

Rasher eased his revolver back into its hip holster. "I mean you no disrespect, Mr. Capuzzi. But while this may be your place of business, this business between Mr. Vint and myself has nothing to do with you."

Papa laughed gently; his eyes seemed to twinkle. "Ah, but as a community leader, so *much* 'personal business' is also my business. You see, I'm something of a . . . coordinator, Stanley. Sorting out, sometimes, the conflicting desires of the so-called straight world and the underworld . . . and that twilight world of police and politicians that lies between."

"I fail to see how serial killings relate to any of what you're saying."

Papa shrugged. "We each have our place in the City. We're all swimming in the same waters. Our crime rate is relatively low . . . thanks to the help of boys like you, Stanley, God bless you. We all have our place, we all have our role, and in a way we all work together. More closely, sometimes, than others. That's why we're workin' together on this Taurus thing."

"Together?"

Papa nodded.

Rasher glanced at Vint, then back to Papa. "You say that like you're *sure* it's this bastard Taurus who's killing these girls."

"Stanley," Papa said, patting the air, "please. Watch your language. This is a family restaurant."

Rasher turned back to Vint and glared. "How the hell do you fit in? And just who the hell *are* you?"

"I'm a cop," Vint said. "I just don't work for the FBI."

"He's a trouble-shooter," Papa said, genially. "A private eye with one client."

"And I know who that client is," Rasher said, standing, throwing down his napkin like a gauntlet. "You're a fucking mob button man, and I'm having none of it."

"Please, Stanley!" Papa said. "The f-word!"

And Rasher stormed out.

Papa looked at Vint and shrugged with frustration.

"I'll handle it," Vint said.

"Don't kill Stanley," the old man said. "He's a nice boy."

Vint wiped his hands on the napkin.

"Try not," he said.

At headquarters, Vint leaned across the counter at Records and Identification: no sign of Melissa, her computer station empty, though it wasn't yet six.

"Melissa around?" Vint asked one of her co-workers, a pleasant heavy-set woman in her twenties with Annie hair that was not only out of style, it never should have been in.

"She took off early," was the perky response. "She's got that pageant reception, at the country club tonight?"

The Rasher family home was in a blue-collar neighborhood in Irish Town, a clapboard bungalow with a well-tended lawn and a screened-in porch; from conversation with Melissa, Vint knew she and her brother shared the place. He knocked at the screen door, got no answer, went onto the porch, knocked on the front door, which was ajar; his knock opened it enough to reveal Rasher sitting in a living room whose furnishings dated to the 1950s.

The detective was slowly, methodically, loading his handgun.

Vint planted himself before the man he considered to be his partner and stated his case: "I *am* a cop—just like you. The world needs us both. People step outside the rules, we make 'em step back inside. One way or the other."

Rasher put another bullet in the gun; his hands were unsteady, but he was getting it done.

Making speeches made Vint uncomfortable, but this was a speech that needed making.

He said, "Michael Rose—Taurus—is the son of Francesco Roselli—West Coast capo. Twenty years back, we got to the sick bastard before the cops. I should've buried him in the ground. Instead I gave him to his poppa and they buried him out here. In the anonymity of your great big city. Gave him a new life. Made him clean up his act."

Rasher looked up.

"He kept his pecker in his pants for a long, long time," Vint said. "The first firecracker kill made some alarm bells go off. That's when the Commission rushed me in to check up on sleeping beauty. To see if he woke up. Which he obviously has. Well, it's time to put him to sleep again—permanently. You want to help or not?"

Speaking with some difficulty, Rasher said, "The bastard has Melissa."

"What?"

"See for yourself." Rasher holstered the loaded gun, stood and strode up the stairs to Melissa's room, Vint following. The nightstand lamp was on the floor, in pieces; perfume bottles and jewelry had been knocked from her mirrored dresser. But this wasn't the aftermath of a robbery: the drawers of the bureau were shut tight. These were the signs of a struggle.

And the artist had left a variation of his distinctive signature: in the middle of the floor was a pair of Melissa's panties, wrapped in a firecracker.

"We can call this in," Vint said, "and get a mobile crime lab in here. . . ."

"Or we can save my sister," Rasher said.

The protective gate was down, at the front of the Rose Photography Studio, but Rasher kicked a door in, the alley door in back, and found the place empty. The same was true of the apartment above, where Michael Rose lived. The place was tidy, furnishings cold and modern.

But under the false bottom of a dresser drawer, Rasher turned up a hidden cache of photos—more photos of the two dead girls.

Carrying them in a handkerchief, Rasher took them down to the studio, which Vint was searching.

"Before and after photos," Rasher said, displaying the bondage-style shots.

"Alive and dead, you mean. Take a look at this."

Vint opened an album of photos; within were the candidates for the Miss Independence Day competition, to be held the next day at the Mardi Gras-like Fourth of July Festivities on the waterfront.

"I'll be go to hell," Rasher said numbly. "He's the official photographer for the pageant. . . ."

"Keep going."

In back of the album were two more photos, studio portraits of two attractive teenage girls who looked disturbingly familiar.

The two firecracker kills.

"This," Vint said emotionlessly, "is a photo album of his victims . . . the ones he's already killed, and the ones he's *going* to kill . . ."

As if confirming this theory, Vint turned the pages of the

book Rasher held to its final page, a photo of Melissa, mouth taped shut, eyes taped open.

"Print's still damp," Vint pointed out.

Rasher was trembling with rage and fear. "He killed one girl on the first of July, another on the second, and now it's the third and he's got Melissa."

"Obviously, tomorrow he plans to hit the rest of these girls," Vint said. "A sniperscope aimed at the stage, perhaps."

Rasher was reeling. "Why, after all these years, is Taurus launching such an orgy of slaughter?"

"There's one last photo you need to see," Vint said. "Actually, it's a negative. . . ."

Vint nodded to a light box where he had already displayed a large chest X-ray.

Rasher, as confused as he was worried, stumbled over and said, "What the hell's this about?"

"You don't have to have a medical degree to see the spots on those lungs. Of all the pictures in this studio, this one—the only one here that Michael Rose didn't take himself—tells us the most."

"Cancer?"

Vint nodded. "Taurus is dying."

And the meaning, the intent behind the orgy of slaughter was suddenly all too clear in Rasher's mind.

"Oh God," Rasher said, feeling like he'd been struck a blow in the pit of his stomach. "Taurus believes that each of his victims will be his slave in the next world . . ."

Vint nodded. "So he's collecting as many pretty young souls as he can before he cashes in."

"We have to find him tonight," Rasher said, intensely. "Not just Melissa's life is at stake, but think of those girls on that festival stage tomorrow, and all the people in the audience who could get caught in a crossfire between that madman and the SWAT boys."

Vint shook his head, no. "He won't hit the festival tomorrow."

"But everything points to that . . ."

"Taurus is a madman, but he's no fool. By now, he knows we'd be on top of him, at the festival. He'll change his plans . . . but not his goal."

Rasher snapped his fingers.

"The reception for the beauty pageant contestants," the detective said, "is going on right now . . ."

"Not a bad guess," Vint said. "Let's drop by the country club . . ."

"I'll take time for one phone call, first," Rasher said, and he used his cellular and caught Lt. Price at the 32nd.

"We were checking up on a suspect in the firecracker killings, Lieutenant," Rasher said, after giving Price the location. "And we found the rear door kicked in. Apparently a break-in . . ."

"Ah," Price said, not fooled, but happy to go along.

"We're seeking the suspect elsewhere—there's a time factor involved—so get a unit over here. There's a counter in the photo studio where we'll be leaving some key evidence you'll need to bag and inventory."

"Evidence?"

"Items we discovered in plain sight, when we were checking up on that robbery."

"Ah," Price said again. "My people will be on it. Go do what you gotta do."

Vint parked his Porsche along the roadside, in the shadow of a rolling hill, and soon he and Rasher were moving under the clear starry sky across the country club's golf course, shadows slipping quietly along, guns in hand. As they approached the dome of Starview Observatory, they came across a Ford van parked up off the graveled lot, by the bushes; the lettering on the van said ROSE PHOTOGRAPHY. The van was locked, but on tiptoes, looking up through the windshield, they could see the vehicle was empty.

Cautiously they approached the observatory. In an open window high in the domed structure, something glinted.

The metal of a gun?

A sniper's scope?

Vint clutched Rasher's arm. "You got to get those people out of that country club—out the front way. He has a view of the veranda from up there, but not of the front of the place."

"No, you go," Rasher whispered harshly. "*I* want to take him. . . . He may have Melissa in there. . . ."

"That country club is packed with prominent locals," Vint said. "They know you. They'll do what you tell 'em."

Rasher sighed, nodding his reluctant agreement. He bounded across the golf course, toward the country club, staying low, staying along the bushes and trees of the rough.

Vint entered the observatory through the main door, walking across the echo chamber of the marbled lobby as quiet as a whisper. He moved through the dark building slowly, past exhibits, skirting a large model of the moon, heading into the cavern of the planetarium, circling around the massive telescope's base, listening to every sound, every creak.

Then he spotted the dark shape up on the observatory platform.

Carefully, silenced automatic in hand, Vint began to climb the stairs. . . .

Inside the country club, various city fathers were honoring the lovely young women with their presence, as the potential

Miss Independence Day's in their beaming smiles and prom gowns circulated among the crowd at this well-attended reception. Rasher quickly tried to ascertain who was in charge.

"Detective Rasher, isn't it?"

Rasher turned and was facing Hiram Goldman, smiling above the rim of a martini glass. Slender, handsome, looking like he stepped off the top of a wedding cake, Goldman was the city's latest financial golden boy, a society page favorite and a pillar of this country club which, only a few decades ago, wouldn't have allowed in a member of his "persuasion."

The self-confident Goldman seemed perpetually amused. "Don't tell me my wife's jewelry has finally turned up?"

"I've been off robbery detail for two years, Mr. Goldman, but I am glad to see a familiar face."

The darkly handsome financier lost his smirky smile, obviously sensing Rasher's urgency. "Why?"

"Mr. Goldman," Rasher said sotto voce, "we've got a bad situation. . . . I want you to help me get all of these people out of here and away from the building, right now."

"Don't be silly," Goldman said. "We have a fireworks display in half an hour. Everyone's looking forward to it. . . ."

"Mr. Goldman, the man who's behind the firecracker kills is out back with a sniper-scope, looking for more pretty girls to murder. What do you suppose will happen, when the pageant contestants go out on the veranda to watch the fireworks?"

"Understood," Goldman said, and moving casually through the crowd, revealing no sense of urgency whatever, the financier found his way to where a small combo was playing and calmly commandeered a microphone.

"Thank you for coming tonight," he told a crowd that had quieted immediately, seeing who it was that was speaking to them. "All of us on the pageant committee are grateful for your support, but it's my unhappy duty to call a temporary halt to these festive proceedings. There's a minor gas leak and the building has to be evacuated."

Murmurs of disappointment moved across the room in a wave.

"But I will call ahead and arrange a banquet room at Le Figaro, where we can continue this party at my expense."

Now the murmur turned into approval, and then applause.

As the guests, pageant contestants among them, began filing out, with no trace of panic thanks to Goldman's efforts, the financier turned to Rasher and said, "Would you go out back, and tell the technicians mounting the fireworks show that their performance should be temporarily postponed?"

"I'll take care of it," Rasher said. "Just point me in the right direction. . . ."

In the observatory, on the platform, Vint approached the stocky figure, who was dressed entirely in black, a chubby cat burglar, aiming a sniper-scoped rifle out a window.

"Planning to gather a few slaves, Michael?"

And Michael Rose turned, revealing a big boyish smile and a shirtfront bearing a homemade rendering in glitter paint of the astrological symbol of Taurus the Bull.

"Vint! I'd hoped you come." He chuckled, eyes glittering behind the wire frames. "Miss Independence Day is going to miss her independence, when she and her court serve me for eternity. Maybe you'd like to my servant in the next world, too."

"Maybe you'd like to kiss my ass in this one."

Michael laughed, a childish giddy laugh that echoed through the observatory. "Maybe you'd like to kiss yours goodbye, Vint. You should know that Taurus always triumphs."

"You were born under the sign of Taurus," Vint said, taking a step forward. "But you're dying under the sign of Cancer."

Michael frowned, and said, "Where's your policeman friend?"

"Stealing your slaves away. All your victims have been warned, by now. They're gone. Now, put the rifle down, slow."

Michael seemed to be considering that, then he shrugged and bent at the knees to lower the rifle to the platform floor. "Okay, Vint—you win. As usual." Then he straightened and smirked and said, "Of course, one slave's still available to me . . . your friend's sister. The love of your sad life? I saw you two, together, you know."

Vint raised the gun and pointed its silenced snout directly at Michael's forehead and said, "You're going to be *my* slave in the next world, asshole."

Michael opened his palm and revealed a small device, a push-button remote control. "Then say good-bye to Melissa . . . asshole."

Vint, finger poised on the trigger, paused.

"Where is she, Michael?"

"And if I tell you, you'll let me live?"

"Maybe."

"But Vint, you said it yourself . . . I'm dying already. I'd rather have one more slave and die right now then be hauled off to jail or the nuthouse and never claim any more loyal subjects. . . ."

Out on the golf course, outside the supply shed that had been appropriated for the fireworks show, Rasher had stumbled upon the two technicians who were supposed to set off the country club fireworks show. They were lying down on the job—their throats slashed. The detective stood staring at the door of the shed, wondering if his sister was in there, hoping the damn thing wasn't booby-trapped. . . .

In the observatory, on the platform, Vint trained his nine-millimeter on the seemingly amused Michael Rose.

"She's tied up in the fireworks shed," Michael said, giggling, "wired to some real *big* firecrackers. And if I press this little button, she'll go all to pieces."

"Then press the button," Vint said, calmly. "Only if you do, Michael, I'm going to kill you slow. . . . I'll put one in your fat gut and let you wallow in pain; then, just to keep you alert, I'll shoot your kneecaps off, and shatter your elbows. It'll be hours of agony before you go to your well-deserved hell."

"I don't think you'll do that," Michael said.

"Try me."

"When my daddy learns you didn't put me out of my 'misery' quickly, he'll be very mad. I think you'd be the one learning how slow a man can die."

The pudgy bastard had a point.

"Then here's what we're going to do," Vint said. "We're going to walk down the steps and out of here, slowly. You're going to lead me to where you have Melissa. And you're going to let her go."

Michael frowned and laughed. "Why should I?"

The gun was still trained on Michael's forehead, but Vint's voice was almost soothing as he said, "Because if you do . . . and if you behave . . . I'll keep you away from the cops. I'll turn you over to your daddy, the don, alive. He can find some new rock to hide you under, until God kills you."

Childishly, Michael repeated, "Why should I?"

"Because if you don't, I'll take my chances with trying a head shot. You won't have time to press that button. A head shot kills all reflexes, Michael."

"What if I fall on this thing?" Michael said, holding the

detonator in front of him.

"You might," Vint conceded. "That's why I'm offering you an option."

Michael thought about it; then, grinning like the goofy kid he was, he nodded, saying, "Okey dokey."

But even as Vint and his hostage were abandoning the observatory and heading toward the fireworks shed, Rasher was inside the little structure, untying Melissa, who he found in bra and panties, bound in a seated bondage position, mouth taped shut, eyes open wide. She sat in the midst of fireworks of all kinds—roman candles, rockets, piles of pyrotechnics waiting to paint the night. She seemed to be trying to convey something with her expression to Rasher, but he picked her up as gently as he could and carried her over to a practice putting green and eased her to the grass.

He removed the taped gag and she said, "I was afraid you might set that thing off!"

"What thing?"

"He's got that shed loaded up with dynamite and wired to blow. . . . We've got to get away from here!"

Rasher finished removing her duct-tape bonds, draped her in his suit coat, and walked her around to the front of the evacuated country club.

"Can you do me a favor?" he asked his sister.

The brutalized young woman managed a nod.

"Call 911. Get me some back-up. Then stay inside that building and don't come out till you hear help come."

She nodded, and he guided her inside, and headed back onto the golf course.

Vint and Michael Rose had arrived at the fireworks shed, having walked side-by-side from the observatory, in a Mexican stand-off, Vint's gun trained on Taurus, who continued to hold the detonator, thumb poised to press.

"Where is she?" Vint demanded, as both men looked in the open door of the shed that was filled with fireworks but empty of Melissa.

"I've got her, Vint!" Rasher called out, from behind him, seeing Vint with a gun trained on Taurus, assuming the latter was Vint's prisoner. "She's safe!"

When Vint half-turned toward the sound of Rasher's voice, Michael Rose struck out, ramming a fist into the side of Vint's face. Vint went down, his gun tumbling from his fingers and Taurus scurrying into the night.

Rasher—knowing nothing about the dangerous detonator in Taurus' grasp—took off after the man, and threw a flying tackle into him, taking him down, hard, sending the detonator flying, Rose rolling out of Rasher's grip on the slope.

Michael lumbered to his feet. So did Rasher. And in the moonlight, under the starry sky, in the cool air that had followed the hellish hot day, Taurus the Bull threw a punch into Rasher the bull, whose return blow broke his opponent's jaw.

But the bloody-mouthed Taurus, eyes glittering (the wire frames had been lost in the tackle), moved in with flailing yet powerful blows that sent Rasher backward, reeling. The detective's more skillful, more measured blows caused Taurus to stagger, and as the insane slugfest careened across the course, the two men were soon back where they started, trading blows near the open door of the fireworks-filled shed.

Vint was on his feet now, and while the brutal hand-to-hand combat continued between cop and killer, the private detective who worked for the mob calmly recovered both his gun and the detonator.

"Enough of this shit," Vint said to nobody in particular,

and he went over to the two men who were struggling on the ground now, Taurus on top, his heavier weight giving the momentary advantage.

Vint hauled Michael Rose off Rasher as easily as if he were picking a flower and hurled the son of a bitch into the fireworks shed, slamming the door, latching it, snapping the Yale lock shut. Taurus, within the shed, was pounding the walls, the structure shaking with his indignation.

Vint dragged Rasher up off the ground and away from the shed, back into the night, across the golf course, toward the observatory, well away from the little structure that shook with Taurus' rage.

"What the hell are you doing?" Rasher demanded, groggily. "I wanted to take that bastard in, personally!"

Vint smiled gently, put his hand on Rasher's shoulder and said, "It's after midnight. Do you know what that means?"

"What . . . ?"

"Happy Fourth of July, Stan."

And Vint pressed the detonator.

A yellow ball of flame rose heavenward, followed by the millisecond afterthought of the roar of the explosion, and fireworks begin to fill the sky, sparkling bursts, skyrocketing streaks, in glorious celebration.

Rasher stared with wide eyes into the patriotic sky, stunned at first, and then he began to smile. "I thought you didn't like noise," Rasher said, turning.

But Vint was gone.

And Rasher stared into the darkness of the rough, wondering if he should go into the bushes and trees after Vint, who was, after all, nothing but a mob hit man. And wasn't Rasher a cop?

Then, slowly, Rasher began to smile again.

Shrugging, laughing, he looked up at a heaven filled with

fireworks, a night alive with whistles and pops and bangs, and put his hands in his pockets, and walked toward the clubhouse, under an exploding sky.

The bottom line was, Vint had made a hell of a partner.

And that was no bull.

THANKSGIVING

A Bird for Becky

Sooner or later, in the life of a private eye in the city, a beautiful woman with a problem walks in the door; and two days before Thanksgiving of 1943, on a delightful fall afternoon in Chicago, a soot-tinged but nonetheless pleasant breeze breathing in the window riding the coattails of the elevated train rumbling by, that is exactly what happened to Richard Stone.

He just didn't expect her to be thirteen years old and the sister of his fiancée (and secretary).

"Katie isn't here, kid," said Stone, the rangy, darkly handsome detective. "It's her afternoon off."

He was twenty-nine years of age and fit as a fiddle but hadn't fought in the war; he was one detective who really did have flat feet. Moderately successful, he did mostly retail-credit checks, after finally getting disgusted with divorce work. A snappy dresser, his ten-dollar green-and-black tie loose at the collar of his brown double-breasted gabardine, he had just lighted up an Havana cigar having finished up a stack of reports when he heard somebody entering out in the outer office, followed by the little knock at his inner office door.

"I know it's Katie's afternoon off," Becky said, peeking in the barely opened pebbled-glass-and-wood door, her voice as tentative as it was sweet. She was a cherubic child, china-doll pretty, round-lensed wire glasses perched on her button nose lending her an air of studiousness, honey-blonde red-

ribboned hair brushing her shoulders. "I was with her—I . . .
I'm afraid I ditched her at the department store."

"That's no way to treat your big sister," he said, trying to
put a little scold in his voice, but liking her spirit—and, like
any good detective, curious as to her motives.

The child entered the room—and she was a child, a
slender teenage beauty barely touched by puberty's hand—
and he felt almost guilty noticing how nice her legs were as
they flashed toward him under the blue pleated skirt. Her
blouse of blue with white stripes had parallel rows of tiny
white buttons that gave her a naval air.

Her expression was military-severe, too, as she positioned
herself before his desk; so was her posture. An ex-soldier
might have said, "At ease."

Stone said, "Sit down, honey. Take a load off."

She pulled up the client's chair and sat, but she remained
troubled, a furrow digging into that smooth, smooth brow. "I
need your advice, Uncle Dick. Your help."

"You know you can come to me for me anything, doll-
face. Unless you've gone and found another guy on me?"

Now she smiled. "No. You're still my best beau, Uncle
Dick."

"Good. So what's the trouble? What's got you shakin' off
your sister in the middle of Christmas shopping?"

Becky and Katie lived with their widowed mother in a
Northside apartment. The child was on Thanksgiving vacation break.

She was frowning in thought. "I think I need to see an
alienist. Or is psychiatrist the more accepted term now?"

He resisted the urge to smile. If anybody was well ad-
justed, it was this kid; if any thirteen-year-old didn't need a
head shrinker, it was her. She used proper English, went to
church (and Sunday school) with perfect-attendance-pin reg-

ularity, wore no make-up despite peer pressure, was a voracious reader, and earned straight A's. Her nastiest habit was buying movie fan magazines and taking in two picture shows every weekend.

He played it straight, however; didn't kid her.

"What's troubling you, sweetheart?"

Her eyes lowered; they were darting, as if she were following a mouse scurrying around down on the floorboards. "It started last . . . last month. I was doing research at the library."

Some wild kid, this Becky.

Now the big long-lashed eyes raised and locked onto him, unblinkingly blue and beautiful. "You remember . . . that gangster picture you took me to?"

"Oh, hell's bells, kid—you didn't tell your sis we took in that matinee, did you?" He had told Katie they were going to a Disney picture. "She doesn't like that violent nonsense. She'll kill me if she finds out—"

"Remember how you told me," Becky said, rolling over his words, "that *this* city, *our* city, had *real* gangsters a lot, lot worse than anything in that picture?"

"Sure. Right. I told you that movie was a laundered, Hollywood version of a real story. About a real gangster—Moe Kingman."

Fourteen years ago, the city had been rocked with gang wars, and Morris "Moe" Kingman had been in the thick of it; a daring, innovative gang leader, King Moe had worked to form alliances with the Caprices, Greenbergs and every criminal faction from Cicero to Gary, then double-crossed them and wound up riddled with lead in a ditch.

"Well, I went to the library to do research," Becky said. "I read all the old newspaper accounts. And there were magazines articles, too, in the national press, and even a couple books on the subject. . . ."

"Don't tell me you did a term paper on it."

She nodded. "Yes. For social studies. 'Diplomacy in the Criminal Underworld: the Failed Reign of King Moe.' I got an A minus."

"Minus? That's not like you."

She shrugged and her blonde locks bounced. "The 'minus' was for 'inappropriate subject matter.' "

"Ah. So blood and guts doesn't play in eighth-grade Social Studies."

"No. You can get away with it in History, better. You should read my Genghis Khan paper."

"Becky," Stone said, grinning, shaking his head, "you have hidden depths I knew nothing about."

"You can say that again, flatfoot."

Stone blinked; not only were the words inappropriate, coming from that sweet kewpie mouth, but the voice itself was suddenly of a new, deeper, rougher timbre. Almost, not quite, a male timbre: but still, it was a little girl's voice, it was Becky's voice all right. . . .

"Becky?"

"Not Becky," Becky said, and her eyes had narrowed, and her mouth was a sneering smirk. "Name's Moe. But you can call me Mr. Kingman."

Stone's breath drew in, involuntarily; he might have been hit in the stomach.

"Becky . . . what the hell kind of talk. . . ."

"Watch your language, dick," Becky said, the lack of capitalization on the word apparent in her rough, mannish tone. "Don't ya know you're talkin' to a damn kid?"

And Becky chortled. She squinted in irritation and removed the wire glasses, tossing them onto the desk. Then she reached for the brown wooden humidor to the right of his blotter, popped the lid and selected a Havana. Stone's jaw dropped as he watched her use the horse-head lighter on his desk to fire it up.

The child's quick puffs developed into a long draw on the cigar that, finally, made her cough. "Lousy brat's lungs ain't worth beans," then seemed to settle down, puffing on the luxurious smoke, easing back in the chair and crossing her legs in a most unladylike manner, an ankle resting on a knee.

"You know, Beck," Stone said, sitting forward, "I like a good laugh as much as the next guy. But you're pushing it. If your sis . . ."

"She ain't gonna show up here," Becky said. "It's her day off! Why would she comin' look for the brat, here, anyway?"

Stone stood. He pointed a scolding finger. "Put out that damn cigar. Now!"

"Tch tch tch," Becky said, cigar buried in a corner of her mouth, bobbling; the kid's face had transformed into something you might see in a pool hall. "Language! A child is present."

"You're not too big for me to lay you over my knee . . ."

"I think I am," Becky said, looking herself over. "A little flat-chested, maybe, but this is definitely not a body you wanna be layin' over your knee . . . particularly if your secretary fools us and *does* show up."

That froze Stone; not just the threat: but the nasty adult knowledge this kid suddenly had.

"You wanna keep your distance from me, dick," Becky said. "Hands off. Dirty old men go to jail, you know, for takin' advantage of sweet young things. Word 'jailbait' ring a bell?"

Stone was reeling. He stumbled back behind his desk and lowered himself into the swivel chair. "Becky . . . what's this about?"

The sweet kid's face grimaced around the cigar. "I told ya, knucklehead. The name's Moe Kingman. Yeah, yeah—and you can call me Moe. Be my guest."

She had come to him talking about a psychiatrist; and as he looked into the cold narrow eyes in the child's face, Stone knew this was not a joke. This was something. Something strange. Something terrible. Something real.

Becky was batting the air with a hand in which the cigar was propped, making smoke trails. "Listen, I don't know much about this mumbo jumbo . . . ask the kid, when she comes back. I know *she's* got a theory. Jeez, kind of an egghead, don't you think?" Becky gestured to herself. "Good lookin' kid like this, and no boy friend? She oughta be hangin' around the soda shop, lookin' for partners to play post office—not hauntin' the library, researchin' dead gangsters."

"Like you."

"Like me. Look—here's where the kid comes in. For whatever reason, she's the door I found to come through. I been asleep for God knows how long . . . or maybe the damn devil knows. Anyway—I'm back. I'm in her head, and talkin' through her mouth. Get the picture?"

"Starting to."

"I'd rather have my old body back, but last time I looked it was full of holes. Worms are crawling in and out of them holes, about now, and makin' new ones."

"Probably not, Moe. You're dust and bones by now."

"Rub it in, why don't you? Now here's where you come in—you're gonna find my killer."

"What?"

Becky's grin was in no way girlish. "Find my killer, and I'll give you the kid back. Or at least, I'll try to. I'd be lyin' if I said I was in complete control of this situation."

"Don't you know who killed you?"

"Sure, in the who-pulled-the-trigger sense. It was Duke Mantis. That bum still around?"

Stone nodded. "Sure. Running your old club, the Palace . . . only it's called the Chez Dee now, after the current owner, Danny O'Donnell. Only, Duke doesn't get his hands dirty anymore."

She snorted. "He was a cheap gunsel back when I knew 'im. Smalltimer, freelance, not aligned with nobody. And before he plugged me, the slob didn't do me the courtesy of tellin' me *who* hired 'im—and who *framed* me."

"Framed you?"

"Yeah. I had a counsel meeting organized, bringin' every outfit together into one big syndicate. And somebody made me out a double-crosser. Some damn Judas in the woodpile. *That's* who really killed me. . . ."

Becky touched her chest; her face seemed greenish.

"Jeez Louise," she growled. "Maybe this thing's a little strong for me, after all that time away. . . ."

She rested the cigar in his glass ashtray and then, like a child at school resting her head on her desk, rested hers on his. Stone rose, came around and stroked the sleeping child's head.

He stood there watching her slumber, her breathing building to a gentle snore, and wondered how he could help her. She was his client, after all. Wasn't she in his client's chair?

The door in the outer office opened and he heard Katie call out: "Richard! Richard, I need your help!"

He went out to her, Katie Crockett, his sandy-haired secretary (and fiancée), her lovely dark eyes brimming with tears, her high-cheekboned model's features clenched with worry.

"I can't find Becky anywhere," she blurted. "We were

shopping and I just turned around and—"

"She's right here, sweetheart," he said, taking her by the arm; the young woman wore a gray woolen coat with shiny brass military buttons over a white blouse and navy skirt. "She got lost and was pretty worried, herself . . . and when she couldn't find you, she came here looking for me. Knowing you'd check here eventually."

By this time Katie, listening as she went, had moved into the inner office where she could see the child sleeping, head on the desk. The smell of cigar smoke hung like a nasty curtain, however, and Katie's face—which had gone from worry to relief in a heartbeat—now turned to a frown.

"Richard—were you smoking one of these in front of her?"

"No. No, sweetheart . . . I just happened to be smoking when she came in. I put it right out."

"That awful smoke. So strong. Bad for her."

"I couldn't agree more."

Now Katie clung to his arm, fell against him, her coiled worry having turned completely to loose-limbed relief. "Thank God she looks up to you so. And thought to come here."

"She's a great kid."

"The best. But lately . . ."

"What?"

"I don't know," Katie said, and her shoulder-length locks bounced on her shoulders, much as Becky's had earlier. "She just . . . hasn't quite been herself lately."

Private First Class Ben Crockett, Katie's younger brother, Becky's older brother, had died in the war. The news had come last Christmas—a Christmas day telegram that had brought anything but good cheer—and now with the holiday season upon them again, Ben's family would have bittersweet memories to deal with, with the bitter almost certainly out-weighing the sweet. Stone knew that Becky adored her brother and was hardly surprised the girl was troubled.

But for those troubles to emerge in such a bizarre fashion was unexpected, to say the least.

He took Katie and her sister out for supper, the Bismarck Hotel's dining room where the menu was "Bavarian" (before the war, it had been German). Dark wood, rich carpet, glittering glass chandeliers, mirrored walls that made the large room huge and of course linen tablecloths provided an elegant evening-out atmosphere that he hoped would soothe both his girls. And anyway, the chef was a client and a pal and the bill would be on the cuff.

But nobody—not even Stone—finished their fancy meals; a gray cloud hung over the table: Katie's stomach was "nervous" from the scare of losing Becky at the department store; and the child and the detective stole furtive glances as they shared their terrible secret.

When Katie went to the powder room, way off in the hotel lobby, the detective and his client were finally alone.

"When did this start?"

"Today was the first time, Uncle Dick. The first time he . . . came out."

"What do you mean, 'came out'?"

She shrugged helplessly. "Before this, he was just a voice in my head. Talking to me. Sometimes out loud, in the mirror, but with nobody around. Except for, well . . . several times he . . . he took over, and pretended to be me."

"Pretended?"

She nodded, blonde locks bobbing, blue eyes bright and worried behind the round lenses. "But he wasn't very good at it. He used slang words I wouldn't. Sis gave him . . . or me . . . some awful funny looks."

"You know . . . your idea about seeing that certain kind of doctor. It ain't a bad one."

Another nod, the eyes widening. "Hearing voices is a symptom of certain mental illnesses. I did research on a paper for . . ."

"I'm sure you did. But this isn't school, Beck. This problem isn't . . . abstract."

She sighed a world-weary sigh beyond her years, and stared into her crystal glass of shaved-ice and water. "Joan of Arc heard voices," she offered, just a little bit defensive about it. "And she was a saint."

Or a screwball with religion, he thought. But he said, "That's right."

"It was his idea, you know."

"Whose idea to what?"

She pointed to her head. "Him. To come see you."

"Moe Kingman sent you to see me? See, there's proof this is your imagination at work, your whadyacallit . . ."

"Subconscious acting up."

"Yeah, that. I wasn't a detective back in Moe Kingman's day—I was a kid, like you. He wouldn't know me from Adam—"

She was shaking her head, no. "He knows everything I know, Uncle Dick. He has my memory to look things up in—like the card catalogue at—"

"The library, I know. Where you get all your great ideas."

She used a fork to traces lines in the tablecloth; quietly, almost pitifully she said, "I hope I *am* crazy."

"Don't talk nonsense."

She looked up and the eyes were wet, now. "I do. I hope I'm fruity as a cornucopia basket, Uncle Dick. I don't wanna be some reincarnated gangster!"

People at nearby tables were looking at them; he shot them

glares, sending them scurrying back to their food as he scooted his chair closer to the kid.

"Moe *said* you had a theory," Stone said quietly, almost whispering. "Is that it?"

She nodded. "Mr. Kingman died about the time I was born. He came back as me, only usually in reincarnation, you don't remember former lives. . . ."

"Ah. So you're an expert on reincarnation, too."

"That history paper I did on King Tut last year? It kind of got me interested. And I also did one for Science called 'Psychic Phenomenon—a Factual Basis for the Supernatural.' And then in Geography my term paper was on 'Religion in India'. . . ."

"Oh, brother. . . ."

"That movie you took me to, and the research . . . must have triggered it. Woke him up, kind of."

Stone humored her. "Well, then—how do we put your former self back to sleep?"

She reached a small delicate hand out and gripped his hand with strength worthy of a steelworker. The eyes behind the glasses were narrow again.

"Find the rat bastard that killed me," Becky said harshly, "and you can have the damn kid back."

Stone blinked and was looking back into the wide eyes of his future niece.

"I'm sorry, Uncle Dick," she said, and she began to cry.

He handed her a linen napkin. "It's okay, baby. Don't worry about it. I'm on the case."

Katie was approaching and Stone told the kid to dry her eyes and pull herself together. Their red-jacketed waiter soon arrived to offer up dessert, but Becky wasn't interested.

"You two have some if you like," she said. "It's my turn to use the restroom."

And as she scurried off—maybe to finish that cry of hers—her older sister said, "You see that, Richard?"

"What?"

"No dessert. She really *isn't* herself."

"The question is," Stone said over a beer in a booth at the Blue Spot, "do I tell Katie?"

"Why wouldn't you tell her?" Hank Ross asked, over his own beer. The heavy-set homicide sergeant, ten years older than Stone, was probably the detective's best friend, and could be counted on for no-nonsense advice.

"I don't know if she can handle it," Stone said. "I've caught her at her desk, bawling over her brother's picture, half a dozen times the last three or four weeks."

Hank smirked, making his bulldog puss even more wrinkled. "You figure Katie's too fragile."

"Something like that."

"Hell, if she can put up with a selfish lunkhead like you for a boss . . . and a boyfriend . . . she can take almost anything."

"Thanks for the vote of confidence. But there's something else."

"What?"

"Becky came to me not just as her 'uncle,' but seeking my help in . . . a professional capacity."

"As a client, you mean."

"Yeah. And she deserves her privacy."

"Client confidentiality kinda thing."

"Right."

Hank's eyes rolled like slot-machine lemons. "Are you completely nuts? Katie's thirteen-year-old sister thinks she's a dead gangster, and you wanna respect her privacy? She needs help, Stoney. Medical help."

"She did bring up the idea of a psychiatrist herself . . ."

"Right. Cook County has a good man on the staff, I can refer ya to; it's who the p.d. uses when any of our own starts developin' belfry bats."

"Hey! This is a normal, well-balanced kid, Hank—"

"Yeah, yeah. Who just happens to think she's the late Moe Kingman. King Moe! That pipsqueak pretender."

"You knew him?"

"I knew him. Five feet six with an ego bigger than a battleship. Pinstripe suits with black shirts and white ties, thirty-dollar Florsheims, puffin' cigars longer than pool cues and costly as a porterhouse."

"Any extra charge for the mixed metaphors?"

Hank laughed over the rim of his beer mug. "Who taught ya that word, that bookworm kid? She's broke up over her brother's death, her overactive imagination is brimmin' with all that hooey from books and movies, and she's a candidate for the laughing academy if you don't get her some help. Client! Jesus!"

"Who murdered Moe Kingman, Hank?"

"Whadda you care? It's ancient history."

"I'm doing research. And I ain't the library type."

Hank let some air out. "Well, the way street scuttlebutt had it, it was Duke Mantis—he was a trigger back before he became a nightclub entrepreneur, y'know."

"But who hired him?"

Hank shrugged, took a gulp of suds and said, "Could have been any one the major mobs—the Caprices, the Greenberg boys, O'Donnell's faction. They were all at that damn dinner."

"You mean, there's some truth in that old wive's tale?"

"Yeah, yeah, I know it sounds like a skyscraper of a tall story, but I was in on the investigation with the county coppers, myself." He shook his head, staring down into his empty beer like he was looking for tealeaves to interpret. "Funny. It was just about, what? Fourteen years ago this month."

Stone nodded. "Thanksgiving dinner for the boys."

The story—which Stone had always dismissed as so much malarkey—was that Moe Kingman had invited a high-ranking rep from every mob in the city out for a Thanksgiving peacemaking dinner at a boondocks roadhouse. They were all sitting around the backroom at a banquet table, big-shot tuxedoed thugs swimming in a haze of cigar smoke, pounding down booze, flirting with scantily-clad B-girl waitresses, waiting for Moe when a waiter placed before them a sliver platter with the biggest, most succulent-looking roast turkey anybody ever saw.

According to the much-passed-around yarn, the waiter had presented Mr. Kingman's apologies for his tardiness and said it was Moe's desire that they not let the bird get cold. To go ahead and carve and eat the steaming, fragrant fowl.

Legend had it that the representative of the Caprice gang was the one who began carving the bird, whose stuffing was a delicate mixture of sage, bread crumbs and TNT.

Hank was holding his empty mug up; a passing waitress took it for refilling. Then the homicide sergeant said, "It was the biggest mess I ever saw. Blood. Guts. Not to mention turkey meat. A real slaughter."

"Then how does anybody know what really happened?"

"Duke was there. Sole survivor. He stepped out into the parking lot to get a pack of smokes outa his glove compartment, and the whole damn place blew up behind him."

"Convenient."

"Maybe. At any rate, King Moe's efforts to consolidate the city's underworld factions into one mob blew to smithereens when that turkey exploded. Any gang leader in town mighta put that contract out on him."

"Moe . . . or Becky . . . thinks somebody in his own mob betrayed him."

"Coulda been. His partner, Sam Parr, took over the mob, for all the good it did him. Parr's a crack bookkeeper, but no kinda businessman. When the Prohibition plug got pulled, the Kingman mob under Parr kinda crumbled."

Parr worked for O'Donnell now.

Hank accepted his refilled mug from the waitress and had a sip; his eyes turned sly. "Of course, maybe . . . if it was Parr who framed him, if Moe *was* framed . . . maybe Parr's motives wasn't strictly business."

"Oh?"

"You are young, aren't ya, Stoney? Moe had a beautiful chorus-girl wife . . . Linda LaRue, real name Selma Horshutz, a blonde with curves in places where most dames don't even have places. Least she used to. I hear she's kinda blowsy now, and's back to using 'Selma.' But Parr stuck by her. They even had a kid."

"Greed and love. The two big motives."

Hank leaned forward. "Stoney, you can't be serious. You're not really gonna look into the murder of Moe Kingman. . . ."

"Why not? You cops never solved the case, did you?"

"Tell ya what, Stoney," Hank said, and he dug out a small notebook and stubby pencil from a suitcoat pocket. "I'm gonna write down that head doctor's number. Whether you take that kid there, or sign on for some help yourself, that's up to you. . . ."

"Richard," Katie said, hugging him by the arm, "I'm so pleased you've taken such an interest in Becky."

They were in the reception area of his modest two-room suite of offices, waiting for the child to come back from the washroom off his inner office.

"No big deal," Stone said. "She wants to pick out a Christmas present for her big sis and needs a little help from Santa."

Katie's big brown eyes were lavishing love on him; she was a beautiful girl under any circumstances, but Katie seemed especially radiant today. "Since Ben died . . . and of course Poppa died when Becky was only four . . . having a strong father figure for her to look up to—well, it's very important."

"Hey, she's a cute kid. My pleasure."

She kissed him, a sweet, long kiss, then smiled slyly at him. "It will be. . . ."

Becky came out from the inner office; she wore a light blue woolen winter coat with a hood and a belt that cinched around her not unlike that of the trenchcoat Stone was wearing. It was an adult-looking garment, but her doll's face was that of a child younger than her thirteen years.

"Thanks for the list," Becky said to her sister, referring to a wish list Katie had given the girl to aid her in shopping.

"You hold down the fort," Stone advised Katie as he took the younger girl by the arm and guided her out the door. "We'll be back in time for dinner."

"Let's eat light," Katie suggested, taking her position behind her desk. "Mom's planning a feast for tomorrow and you two better build up an appetite."

Tomorrow was Thanksgiving, of course, but the thought of a roasted turkey only reminded Stone of a certain banquet Moe Kingman had once thrown.

"Do you feel guilty?" Becky asked him, as they walked toward the parking lot where his Chevy coupe was parked, down the block. The air was fall crisp, with more than a hint of winter to come.

"About fooling your sis? Heck, no. I think we're in agreement we don't want to worry her. We'll see what the doc thinks."

Becky had been eager to take an appointment with the psychiatrist over at Cook County, the one Hank Ross had recommended.

"If the doc advises informing your sis," Stone said, opening the rider's side door of the Chevy for her, "we'll fill her in. Otherwise . . ."

"What she don't know won't hurt her."

He looked at her sharply.

She smiled, and giggled, like the kid she was. "Just pulling your leg, Uncle Dick. That was me talking."

He sighed, smiled back, glad that she was feeling good enough about this to joke a little, but not feeling very much like joking himself.

He was cruising through an industrial district when he felt a small hand on his sleeve.

"Hang a right, shamus," Becky said.

"You kidding around again?" he asked, smiling over at the child.

But the smile froze. Becky, wire frames on the seat between them, was training Sadie at him. And Sadie was no lady: she was Stone's .38.

"I got this outa your desk drawer," Becky said, "when the kid wasn't payin' attention."

Stone's hand tightened on the steering wheel, but he kept any reaction out of his face. "Hiya, Moe. Thought you two shared all your secrets."

"We did. But I'm gettin' stronger, pal."

That wasn't good news.

He turned right, into a rundown area that had never recovered from the Depression. Dead warehouses loomed like an industrial Stonehenge. The gun looked huge in her hand, its snout an awful empty eye that stared at him.

"What do you want, Moe?"

"What I *don't* want is my head shrunk. I ain't a mental condition, dick. I'm an old soul in a new carton."

"So you do buy Becky's take on this."

Becky shrugged, sneered; the .38 was steady in her small hand. "Maybe we're just starting to blur into each other, a little. You want me out of her life, and yours, then get crackin' on the case."

"Why don't you keep Becky's appointment, then, and let an expert hear both you *and* the kid talk." Stone kept his voice calm, reasonable. "If you can convince that shrink you're not a mental condition, then I'll gladly take your case."

Becky's chuckle came rumbling out of depths she didn't possess. "No. I know what makes dicks like you tick. Money."

"How are you gonna manage that, Moe? Becky gets thirty-five cents a week allowance, and she pays her meal ticket out of it."

"Pull over."

"Where?"

"There!" She waved the revolver toward a warehouse labeled ACME STORAGE, a mammoth brick structure with boarded-up windows.

Stone pulled up near the front entry. The street was as empty as a Western ghost town; the fall breeze, unable to find any fallen leaves to blow around, settled for scraps of refuse. At Becky's command, Stone got out of the car, and then she was behind him, the steel nose of the rod digging a hole in his trenchcoat, at the small of his back.

Stone, prodded by the girl's gun, headed for the front door.

"That discolored brick to the left of the number," Becky

said. "It's loose. Work at it and it'll pull out."

He did as he was told—and the brick *was* loose, and when he removed it, he found a key in a recession on the other side of the brick. The key opened the front door, and soon the detective and the little girl with the big gun were standing in a huge open space, broken up only by the posts that climbed to the high open-beamed ceiling, and a small wood-and-glass-walled office opposite where they came in.

"Ran a lot of booze outa here in my day," Becky said, her small harsh voice careening off the cement floor and frightening birds nested high in the rafters, sending them flapping. She nudged him with the gun and their footsteps echoed.

"Okay, dick," Becky said. "Step into my office."

No key was required for that. Any furnishings that had once been here were long gone, though an old frayed green carpet covered the floor.

"Yank the carpet back," Becky demanded. "Over in that corner."

Humoring the kid, not wanting to try to take the gun away for fear it might go off and hurt her (or, for that matter, him), Stone pulled back the carpet. A chunk of wood was fitted down into a recession of the cement floor.

"Lift that outa there," Becky snarled.

He did. It revealed a small cast-iron safe with a combination lock.

"Seven right, one left, four right," Becky said.

He turned the dial as directed; and he heard the tumblers fall into place, and the lock clicked open.

Inside the safe were stacks of greenbacks. The hundred-dollar variety.

"Should be a cool hundred gee's in there, flatfoot," Becky said. "Twenty-five of it's for you, if you take my case. Another twenty-five if . . . *when* . . . you solve it."

182

Stone was lifting the bundles of bucks reverently out of their little basement. He piled them neatly on the floor and at staring at the stuff, legs crossed like a kid playing Indian.

"What about the other fifty gee's?" Stone asked.

"That's for the kid's college education," Becky said. "I an, if she's right, and this is my new life, I gotta look out myself, right?"

brary research hadn't led Becky to that warehouse, that brick, not to mention that loose cash. Stone could not oring himself to believe that his fiancée's kid sister was a re-born mobster; but he was capable of believing that hundred gee's, all right.

As far as Stone was concerned, Moe Kingman had a client. They were in the Chevy again, heading out of the industrial district.

"Let's drop in on my old flame," Becky said, lighting up one of Stone's Havanas with a match off a Blue Spot matchbook from his glove compartment; she had apparently pilfered several cigars at the same time she'd lifted his .38 (which she had returned when Stone accepted the twenty-five thousand dollar retainer).

"Linda LaRue, you mean? Mrs. Sam Parr? That's a good place to start, Moe, but I work alone."

"No," Becky said, and puffed at the cigar, getting it going. "I wanna see her. I gotta see her. See, I loved that dame, and that dame loved me. She'd know me anyplace."

Stone gazed at her, agape. "She'll look at a thirteen-year-old girl and see her years-dead boy friend?"

"I got a distinctive personality," Becky said, cigar tilted upward like an FDR cigarette-in-holder, "no matter what the package."

He couldn't argue with that. "You're going to make yourself sick with those things."

"Naw. The kid's gettin' used to me as a houseguest. You know where my old partner and ex-girl live?"

Stone didn't, but a stop at a phone booth and a quick look in the book was all the detective work it took. Mr. and Mrs. Sam Parr and their grade-school-age son lived in an upper middle-class neighborhood in the northwest suburbs—a story-and-a-half oversize bungalow on an oversize well-tended lawn. A driveway rose to a one-car garage; shrubbery hugged the house; a swing set guarded the rear.

"Not exactly a gangland hideout," Stone said.

"Sam's a bookkeeper," Becky said. The tamped-down cigar was in the car ashtray, for later re-firing. "If Sam killed me, it was for love, not money."

"You don't think your 'old flame' could've been in on it?"

"Never," Becky said, with a flounce of her blonde locks. "I got a way with dames."

"Yeah," Stone said, and headed up the walk.

He knocked at the front door, but got no response; listening carefully, he could hear a mechanical whine from inside. Somebody was doing something in there that was a little noisy—vacuuming, maybe.

"Let's try around back," Stone suggested.

The back door stood open, letting out baking smells. The unmistakable aroma of pecan pie tickled Stone's nostrils. He knocked on the open door, sticking his head in.

"Excuse me," he called, over the thrum of the electric mixer.

She heard him at once—the mixer was only on a low speed, as she blended the pumpkin and spices and milk and eggs and sugar—and in the plainly attractive housewife's face remained echoes of the pretty chorus girl she'd once been. She stood at a counter in a moderate-size, very modern kitchen, gleaming white with electric appliances, electric refrigerator, gas range, white-and-black checked linoleum.

"I'm sorry," she said pleasantly over the mechanical whine, "we don't buy from door-to-door salesmen."

Selma Parr, the former Linda LaRue (nee Horshutz), was pleasantly plump, but pushing it; she wore a white-and-blue checker tablecloth of a housedress with a frilly white apron, her dark blonde hair pinned up. The only powder on her face was some stray flour on one cheek.

"I'm not a salesman, Mrs. Parr," Stone said. "I'm a detective. . . ."

She frowned, turned off the mixer; she pointed toward the outside with her wooden, pumpkin-mixture-moistened mixing spoon. "My husband is a legitimate businessman. If you don't have a warrant, I must ask you to . . ."

He stepped tentatively inside, hat in his hands. "I'm not with the police, ma'am. I'm a private investigator. It's about something that happened a long time ago."

Her eyes—big brown, long-lashed chorus-girl eyes in the matronly face—tightened. "I . . . I don't really care to talk about the past. Please go."

Stone sighed. "There's somebody who wants to see you."

Becky stepped inside, looking sweet and innocent in her blue winter coat, the smell of cigar smoke masked by that of pecan pie.

Selma Parr smiled, the automatic response of a mother to a child, any child. "Why . . . what do you want, little girl? Or should I say 'young lady'? Are you with this gentleman?"

"You still got that tattoo with my name on it, baby?" Becky asked. "The heart-shaped one where the sun don't shine?"

And Selma Parr—the former Linda LaRue (nee Horshutz)—fainted dead away, in a pool of her white apron

185

on her black-and-white checked linoleum, mixing spoon limp in her hand.

The detective helped the housewife up from the floor and was guiding her to the kitchen table when they both noticed that the girl was already seated there—and was in that same, folded-arms, asleep-on-her school-desk posture as in Stone's office.

"What . . . is this about?" Selma asked.

"I think the kid gets worn out, after a while," Stone said matter-of-factly. "Being Moe must take a lot of juice."

Selma's eyes were wide. "Being Moe . . . ?"

Becky was slumbering peacefully; gently snoring.

"There's no way to sugarcoat this," he said.

"Sugarcoat what? How could that . . . child know what . . . she knows?"

"I can only tell you what *I* know," he said.

And as the child slept, Stone told Selma the entire story—well, almost the entire story; the part about the money he kept to himself. Old habits die hard.

It took a while and Selma listened quietly, nodding in interest (if not acceptance) of the bizarre tale, and gradually began interspersing housewifely duties during the telling, rising to tend her pecan pie, removing it from the oven and out to cool, filling a pie crust with pumpkin filling, putting that pie in, finally serving herself and Stone cups of coffee.

"You think this poor kid is a nutcase?" Selma asked. She was on her second cup of coffee and smoking a cigarette now, and the chorus-girl side of her was mingling with the mom.

"She's a brilliant child, and troubled over the death of her brother. It was just last year—Christmas—that the telegram came."

"But—how does she *know* these things?"

Stone shook his head. "I'm not sure. Somehow I don't think she read about your tattoo at the library."

Selma winced. "I wasn't a tramp, Mr. Stone. I was with a handful of men in my day . . . and with only one man, after Moe—my husband. Nobody but Sam and my personal physician ever saw that tattoo. . . ."

He sipped the coffee; it was rich and black and good. "Who knows? Maybe there's something to it. Maybe Moe really was re-born as this sweet kid. Whatever the case, he says he'll leave her alone if I can solve his murder."

"Is that how you intend to address this problem, Mr. Stone?"

"At least in the short term. The way she's acting, if I take her to a shrink, they'll lock her up and throw away the key. Hell, they'll bury it."

Selma seemed genuinely concerned as she gazed at the girl. "With this . . . delusion, she might hurt herself. You say she's smoking already. Maybe drinking will be next . . . Moe was a heavy drinker, you know. He's bound to start in again. . . ."

"Listen to yourself, Selma."

She shook her head. "I know. I know. I'm talking like I believe this, myself."

"Do you know anything about Moe's murder, Selma? Anything you didn't tell the cops?"

She seemed more hurt than alarmed by this question. "Moe . . . that child . . . doesn't think *I* had anything to do with it, does he? She?"

"Moe says you loved him."

Her eyes went half-hooded and wistful; cigarette smoke curled lazily up from her fingers. "I did. He was a little guy, but he had a big heart. He came up hard, from the streets, and got involved in the only line of business that was open to him.

He was trying to stop the gang war, trying to bring about an alliance that could end the killing, and pave the way for the rackets to give over to legitimate business. That's why they killed him."

"Why *who* killed him, Selma?"

"Only Duke Mantis knows the answer to that question." She laughed, hollowly. "Funny—Moe's death did bring about a truce, if not an alliance. All the mobs had something in common: they'd all been betrayed by that 'little dirty double-crosser.' "

"Which you don't think Moe was."

"No. He was a straight-up guy, and I loved him."

"You married his partner."

She lifted her chin nobly. "Sam loved Moe like I did. Sam and Moe came up on the same hard streets together; they mighta been brothers. Sam never only took me under his wing 'cause Moe wasn't there to do it anymore."

"Love makes good men do bad things, Selma."

"Not Sam. He's a gentle soul. Ask Moe . . . I mean, ask her."

Becky was stirring. "Oh . . . where . . . are we, Uncle Dick?"

"You don't know, honey?"

Rubbing her eyes, she tried to shake the grogginess off. "No. When he . . . he takes over, I'm starting to . . . black out. Oh, Uncle Dick—I'm frightened!"

He gathered the girl in his arms and was soothing her as she sobbed into his chest. Selma came around and patted the child's shoulder, as well.

"Could I get you a glass of milk, dear? The pecan pie's for Thanksgiving, but I have cookies."

Becky's smile was warm, and embarrassed. "No thank you, ma'am. I'm sorry if I caused you any trouble."

Then the girl stood, straightened her blue coat and said, "Take me home, Uncle Dick. Please."

"Hey, Mom!"

It was a boy's voice, just outside the door, and then he came in, in a hurry, a fresh-scrubbed freckle-faced kid of twelve with a full head of reddish brown hair, a flurry in dungarees and red-white-and-blue plaid shirt, blurting words out on the run.

"Can I go over to Larry's and play trains? His dad just got him this great Lionel . . . sorry. Didn't know we had company."

"This is Mr. Stone, Morris. And this is Becky . . . what was your last name, dear?"

"Crockett," she said, quietly.

"They're old friends of the family," Selma told her son. "Is it all right with Larry's mother, you coming over?"

"Sure!"

"Then go ahead. Just be back for supper."

And the boy was gone.

"Morris?" Stone asked Selma.

"Yes," she said.

Stone nodded, gathered Becky up and soon they were back in the Chevy.

She was putting her glasses back on. "Who was that, Uncle Dick?"

"Selma Parr. You know, Linda LaRue."

"Moe's old girlfriend! Is she a suspect?"

"I don't think so. Not her *or* her husband, either. You don't name your first-born after a guy you killed."

He dropped his thirteen-year-old client off at Katie's mom's apartment. No sign of Moe, since Becky fell asleep at the Parr place.

"Bring your appetite tomorrow," Katie's mom said. She was an attractive woman in her fifties who might have been Katie's sister but for the snow-white hair.

"You bet, Mrs. Crockett. Is that mincemeat I smell?"

"Certainly is," she said sweetly. "Bet that brings back childhood memories."

"Certainly does." He had hated his mother's mincemeat pies.

But he left the apartment house thinking about Thanksgiving, and about Thanksgiving banquets, and an idea merged with a hunch, becoming a full-blown scheme by the time he got back to the office.

He dialed Sgt. Ross at police headquarters.

"You think you could fix me up," Stone asked his friend, "with the private numbers of the top mob guys in town?"

"You mean Danny O'Donnell himself? And Gus Greenberg?"

"And Papa Caprice, too. All of 'em. I don't want to talk to secretaries, either."

"Well, sure, Stoney. . . . What kind of party are you thinking of throwing?"

"A surprise party."

"Who's the honored guest?"

"The host."

The Chez Dee had been a fixture on bustling Rush Street since speakeasy days; in fact, back when it was called the Palace, the restaurant/nightclub had been renowned for hidden doors, sliding panels and secret staircases that gave prohibition agents fits. The Palace had been King Moe's domain; after his death, Sam Parr had sold the joint to Danny O'Donnell.

Sandwiched between a flower shop and an all-night barbershop, the Chez Dee boasted a canopy, a uniformed doorman and a facade of translucent glass-brick behind which glowed the pulse of night life. Its vertical neon sign glowed, as well, a beacon in the pleasantly chilly night, attracting the upper crust of the city's riff raff—the richer gangsters, the more corrupt politicians, gamblers, show people, industry captains with their shapely "nieces," and even occasional tourists looking for color.

Stone handed the hatcheck girl his trenchcoat and fedora, and got a Celluloid token in return; he paused at the velvet rope and waited. It was fairly early—just before six—and the sleek, glass-and-chrome *art moderne* dining room, with its indirect lighting and stylized murals of slender men and women in tuxes and evening dresses, was sparsely populated. The orchestra hadn't taken its position on the stage yet, and it would be hours before scantily clad showgirls began their "Broadway" revue.

"May I help you, sir?" the dinner-jacketed headwaiter asked. He was a burly guy in his thirties who looked more like a bouncer than a waiter, but his diction was good and he was polite enough.

"I'm Mr. Stone. I made the reservation this afternoon, for your private dining room?"

"Ah yes, Mr. Stone. We're ready for you. Your guests should start arriving, when?"

"Seven. It was a last-minute invite for them, as well."

"Our kitchen is ready for you, although our chef wanted to apologize that he couldn't accommodate your request—It's a little embarrassing that you had to have the main course catered in."

Stone smiled, shrugged. "Well, Thanksgiving dinner just wouldn't be right without a turkey—luckily, the chef at the Bismarck Hotel's a client of mine . . . and you know, roast turkey's their specialty. Here's my guest list. . . ."

Stone handed the man a folded sheet of paper.

"This is certainly an, uh . . . elite group," the astounded headwaiter said.

A Who's Who of the city's underworld is what it was.

"I would appreciate it if Mr. Mantis would stop in and say hello, around seven-thirty," Stone said. "I'm sure my guests would appreciate it, too, as I know a lot of these gentlemen are business associates and friends of his. . . ."

"I'll be sure to tell him. I'm sure he'll stop in." His smile was nervous. "You want me to have a man show you the way?"

"No," Stone said. "I can manage."

He wound through the Chez Dee's dimly lighted oval bar, which was doing considerably better business than the dining room; well-dressed men and women were huddled here and there at tiny tables and in snug booths, as the bar's waitresses—in the Chez Dee's trademark French maid outfits, including mesh stockings—served up pulchritude and cocktails.

He checked the private dining room out. A big banquet table dominated the spartanly appointed area, the only decorative touch another mural—this one a cityscape, in the same stylized deco manner—with a door that connected with the kitchen.

Satisfied with the layout, he returned to the bar and found a stool to park himself to wait for his guests to start arriving. Feeling a little nervous and perhaps a tad smug about his plan, he noticed a slender, attractive waitress working the other side of the room, and felt a chill.

"Want somethin', bud?" the bartender asked.

"Yeah," Stone said hollowly. "A double."

"A double what?"

"A double anything. I'll be back for it. . . ."

He crossed the room and walked over to her, and when she turned, almost collided with her.

With the dim lighting, and her heavy make-up, and well-padded bra, not to mention those nice slender legs, Becky made a nice-looking barmaid, for a thirteen-year-old.

"What the hell are you doing here?" they whispered at each other, simultaneously.

Then he guided her by the arm across the bar, and into the private dining room; she was still carrying her drink tray, though it was empty, except for some change. Kid was making pretty good tips for a beginner.

"What's this about?" Stone demanded.

"I'm doin' your job for ya, flatfoot," Becky said. "This is Duke's joint, so I figured I'd look him up."

"Does your sister know you're here?"

"Yeah, sure. Like she knows I stole her make-up and one of her brassieres and half the toilet paper in that dump to stuff it with. Hey, she's kind of built, your girlfriend."

"Don't talk about your sister that way!" Stone's head was spinning; his gangster guests would be arriving momentarily, and here he was with a pubescent racketeer in mesh stockings on his hands. So to speak.

"Aw, she thinks I'm at the library. And, hell, I know my way around this joint better than anybody alive. . . . I planned this club, designed the place. I know ways in and out of here the cockroaches don't."

"And you sneaked into the dressing room the waitresses and showgirls use, and appropriated a costume, and just blended in."

"That's right. I didn't get to the top of the rackets without brains."

"Your brains were found in a ditch out in the country,

193

Moe, scattered around what used to be left of your head."

"Tell me about it! Just let me get that Duke alone, and I'll get who hired him out of him. . . ."

"How?"

Becky shrugged. "I'm pretty, ain't I? And young. And Mantis is a dog, like all men. One way or another . . ."

Stone grabbed the girl's arm. "If you compromise this innocent kid—"

"Hey! I'll just get him in a compromising position and lower the boom. . . . So what the hell are you doing here?"

Stone quickly told her his plan. And his theory.

Becky's eyes were wide with disbelief. "*That's* who you think killed me? Are you kidding?"

"No. You want in on this, to see for yourself, then I'll tell the bartender we want a couple of waitresses to work the room, and request that the cute kid with the nice legs who walks like a dockworker be one of 'em."

"There's nothin' wrong with the way I walk!"

"You got to promise to behave yourself."

Becky grinned. "I'll be a good girl. Got a cigar on ya? It's about time for my break."

By seven-fifteen the room was filled with hard men in black tuxes, the air a blue fog of cigarette and cigar smoke, drink glasses clinking with ice, boisterous conversation forming a cloud of noise. The chair at the head of the table was empty, but the guests had the first course—salad—without the man they assumed was their host.

Stone had, when he called to invite them, told each of his honored guests that he was calling for Duke Mantis. And, so, each of these underworld figures—Danny O'Donnell, his associate Sam Parr, Gus Greenberg, Papa Caprice, and half a dozen others—understood that this Thanksgiving dinner was being thrown by their old friend, Duke.

Along the walls stood the baggy-suited armed guards of the evening, several bodyguards from each of these rival gangster contingencies; right now, an unspoken truce existed between these men. But behind their raucous laughter and confident talk lurked an uneasiness. Perhaps they were all re-membering another Thanksgiving dinner, with an exploding main course.

But Duke wouldn't try anything in his own joint; that would be suicide. Wouldn't it?

Nonetheless, the first bodyguard in—one of O'Donnell's men—had positioned himself at the door and patted ev-eryone down as they came in. No one objected to O'Donnell setting this ground rule of no firearms, and even the body-guards themselves had willingly given up their rods, which lay on a small table in the corner, revolvers, automatics, piled on a linen tablecloth like a bizarre centerpiece.

Stone's gun wasn't among them; he hadn't packed it. But he knew where it was—this time, Sadie wasn't in Becky's pocket, that was for sure. Becky, one of three under-dressed barmaids working the banquet room, didn't have pockets in that satin scrap of a get-up.

"What are you doin' here, Stone?" Danny O'Donnell asked. His tone was cordial but his eyes were ice.

"I don't know this guy," Greenberg said. "I know every-body here but this guy. Who *is* this guy?"

"Leave him alone, he's a good boy," Papa Caprice said. "Him and Jake Marley were partners."

"Oh yeah," Greenberg said. "Marley was a good man. Used to help us out when he was police chief in that little burg out in the boonies. Are you the kid who caught his killer?"

"One and only," Stone admitted.

"Good for you," Greenberg said, and lifted his bourbon

glass in a casual toast. "Now, where's our host, and where's the goddamn food? I'm hungry."

It was another five minutes before Duke Mantis picked up on that cue; understandable, considering he didn't know he was the host.

Duke was tall, rail-thin and angular, sharp sticks well-arranged in the sheath that was his tuxedo; his dark hair was slicked back in the George Raft manner, his eyes pinpricks of bright black in slits beneath slashes of eyebrow, his nose thin and sharp, mouth a wide cut in a long, narrow, high-cheek-boned sunken-cheeked chalk-white face.

"I'm sorry, Mr. Mantis," the bodyguard at the door said. "Host or not, I gotta frisk you. No firearms at the table."

"I never pack in my own joint," Duke said contemptuously, but stood for the frisk. "Whadaya mean, 'host'?"

Danny O'Donnell rose. "You had one of your people call this afternoon, didn't ya? We all got calls like that. Ain't this your party?"

Mantis moved slowly around the table; for such a bony-looking guy, he had a dancer's grace, and his smile was calm, cool. Without sitting, he positioned himself at the head of the table, leaning both hands on the back of the chair.

"I couldn't be happier havin' you here at the club, boss," Mantis told O'Donnell. "Same goes for the rest of you gents—but I didn't invite ya."

"Then it's some kinda set-up!" Greenberg said, and suddenly everybody was getting up, chairs scraping on the floor, fear in the air.

"Gentlemen!" Stone called out, still seated. "Please sit back down, and take it easy. Mr. Mantis didn't throw this shindig—*I* did."

All of the deadly eyes in the room were on him; it wasn't a wonderful feeling. But soon every one of these hard-faced men had taken a seat—except for Mantis.

"You?" Papa Caprice asked. "But why do you misrepresent yourself?"

"What the hell are you doing," Mantis said, "usin' my name?"

"I invited everyone here," Stone said, quietly, "and said that Duke Mantis would be your host. Well, he is. It's his club."

"But you rented the hall," O'Donnell said.

"Yeah."

"Why?"

"Because fourteen years ago, another Thanksgiving banquet was held . . . and many of you in this room lost close friends and business associates . . . even loved ones. You lost a brother, didn't you, Mr. Greenberg?"

Greenberg nodded solemnly.

The door from the kitchen opened, and Stone's pal Rico from the Bismarck brought in the steaming, aromatic turkey on a silver tray. He put in the midst of the table, nodded at Stone and went out.

"I can guarantee you this bird isn't stuffed with dynamite," Stone said, as the men stared at the main course, contemplating that terrible night fourteen years ago. "I had this catered in from the Bismarck, and you know how great their stuffing is."

"Forget the holiday banter," O'Donnell said. "What's the point of *this* banquet?"

"I was hired by an old friend of Moe Kingman. . . ."

"That bastard!" Greenberg said.

Becky, standing just behind Greenberg, frowned and seemed about ready to conk him with her drink tray; Stone shook his head at her, and she let out a breath and faded back into the woodwork.

"I was hired," Stone began again, "to clear Moe's name."

"He was the lowest murderer that this town ever saw," Danny O'Donnell said, so softly it might have been a prayer.

In the background, Becky winced.

"I don't think so," Stone said. "You think Moe gave every mob in town the bird, fourteen years ago, right? Who alone survived that night?"

Mantis slammed a fist on the table. "What are you sayin'?"

Stone said, "I'm asking—who killed Moe Kingman?"

Shrugs and little smiles around the table made it unanimous when Moe's old friend Sam Parr, a small sad-faced bald man, said, "Everybody knows Duke did it."

Stone looked at Mantis, whose white face had reddened.

Mantis said, "I did it, all right. And that's all I'm sayin'. Back when I was a freelancer, when I took a contract, it was between me and the client."

"Very admirable I'm sure," Stone said, "and I won't ask you to betray your sense of integrity, Duke. But I will ask the question: who hired Duke Mantis to kill Moe Kingman? That's the question I want to ask *you*, gentlemen. *Did* anyone in this room hire Duke to kill Moe Kingman? If not, Duke took it upon himself to do that little deed. And if so, why would he do that? Only because he engineered the entire slaughter of your friends, associates and family, to make Moe Kingman someone all of you would want to kill—and himself a hero. Once word got out Duke was the trigger on that job—with every one of you assuming one of the others hired it done—then Duke was aces with everybody. He went from smalltime freelancer, to running this fancy club for you, Mr. O'Donnell."

Face white again, the blood drained out, Mantis said, "You're dead, Stone. I'm comin' out of retirement to take care of you, personally."

"Unless," Stone said, "I'm wrong, and one of you did hire Duke, here . . . maybe you hired him, Mr. O'Donnell. I mean, you're the one who set up him so sweet."

O'Donnell shook his head.

Stone nodded. "I didn't think so. I mean, I'm sure you felt, Mr. O'Donnell, as did so many of you in this room, somewhat indebted to Duke . . . and perhaps because he was the sole survivor of that awful massacre, felt even a certain . . . loyalty to him."

Becky was taking all this in, with eyes that were wide and yet tight, her lipsticked mouth open.

Mantis said, "I was hired by somebody in this room—but I don't rat out my associates. Rest assured."

Stone said, "We're all friends here. No one in this room has any reason to deny hiring Moe's killer . . . unless no one here did. Did you, Mr. Caprice?"

The white-haired patriarch of the Caprices shook his head solemnly, no. So, one by one, did the representatives of every organized crime group in the city.

"I don't have to take this in my own joint," Mantis said, and he walked quickly to the door.

But the skinny one-time hit man took a quick detour to that table of rods and helped himself, filling his hands. Every man at the table, every bodyguard along the walls, turned their eyes on the wild-eyed club manager. The three barmaids—one of whom was Becky—were equally rapt in giving Duke their attention, as he stood with his back to the closed door between the banquet room and the bar, a .45 automatic in one hand, a .38 revolver in the other.

"You guys give me no choice, do you?" he said. "Stone, you son of a bitch—you signed my death warrant tonight. So I'm the only one who can leave this room alive. . . ."

Stone dove for the turkey, shoved his hand between the

bird's legs and found Sadie, where Chef Rico had tucked her. He didn't bother taking the gun out, just lifted his hand off the table, turkey and all, and fired between the seated O'Donnell and Greenberg, the bullet blazing out from where the bird's head used to be.

Mantis slammed back into the door, nailed in the shoulder, dropping both guns as he did. Bodyguards had the guns in hand before Mantis could even think of retrieving them, and the skinny tuxedoed hood slid down the door, a pile of bleeding bones, whimpering. There was noise out in the bar—shouts, and patrons fleeing the gunfire; but nobody tried to come in. A gangland conference in the backroom where gunplay had broken out was not a party anyone was anxious to join.

It was over—or so Stone assumed.

Becky was heading over to Mantis, and she was reaching inside her neckline, and coming out with a little .32 that Stone recognized as the purse gun he'd given Katie for protection. Becky's bra, like the turkey, had been stuffed with firepower.

She stood above the moaning gangster, pointing the gun at his head.

"Now you pay, you rat bastard," Becky said.

Mantis looked up, astonishment mingling with his pain and self-pity. "What . . . what did I . . . ever do to you?"

She crouched and placed the nose of the gun against Mantis' skull. "I'm about to show you. . . ."

"No," Stone said.

Becky didn't take her eyes off Mantis. "Stay outa this, dick—"

The detective crouched beside her, placed a hand on her shoulder. "You don't need to do this. The men in this room, in their own sweet time, will take care of this problem. . . ."

"It's *my* problem. . . ."

"You pull that trigger, you're bequeathing an innocent kid a stigma she'll never overcome. And, Moe—you *are* that kid."

Becky turned away from Mantis, though the nose of the rod stayed put. The beautiful blue eyes might have been Becky's, but Moe still seemed to have a hold on her.

"Moe, give this kid a break . . . give yourself a break. Live a little."

Becky smiled; her eyes teared up. "You did it, didn't you, dick? Found my killer. The other twenty-five gee's you'll find in your bottom desk drawer, by the way."

"Thanks, Moe."

Becky's laugh was deep and hollow. "How the hell was I to know that the guy that killed me . . . was the guy that killed me?"

And Becky collapsed in a little puddle of skimpy satin and mesh stockings.

When he turned, the room was empty. There had been a shooting, after all, and even in a joint like this, the cops would eventually come and there would be questions. So the gangsters and their retinue had gathered their guns and gone out the kitchen way.

Not a bad idea.

He gathered his fiancée's kid sister in his arms and she was slumbering like a baby when he found his own way out through the kitchen, and into the night.

The next afternoon, after Katie's mom served them a sumptuous dinner that included a far more savory turkey than the shot-up bird he'd left behind at the Chez Dee, Stone was relieved to be given a choice between pumpkin pie and mincemeat.

Katie was helping her mother in the kitchen and Stone was kicking back, so full from the feast he was nearly in pain, wondering if the girls would mind if he turned on the radio to hear the game (he had twenty bucks on Notre Dame), when Becky came over and gave him a hug.

"Thank you for everything, Uncle Dick."

"You know, I'm not going to be your uncle, sweetheart. I'm gonna be your brother-in-law."

"I can use a brother."

He hugged her. "I know."

Her eyes, behind the lenses of the wire-frame glasses, were bright and a little sad. "He's gone, isn't he?"

"Ben?"

"No. I . . . I mean Mr. Kingman."

"I think so. Though if you're right about reincarnation, the good qualities he had are still with you."

"You know, I think he left me something. A keepsake."

"What?"

"I'll show you."

She went off to her room and came back with a turkey—a cloth one, a stuffed animal, a toy, a comical looking gobbler like something out of a cartoon. She plopped it on his lap. "Unless *you* bought it for me, Uncle Dick."

He examined the cloth bird. "Can't say I did. You don't remember getting this for yourself, when you were him?"

She shook her head. "No. Toward the end, he just kinda took over. It was like I was . . . asleep."

He examined it; the thing wasn't sewn together very well. In fact, he could see where it had been opened up at its professional seam, and then clumsily, hastily re-sewn. And he saw the corner of something. Something green. Something paper. . . .

"I'm gonna have to open this up, honey," he said. "But we can get it sewn back up. . . ."

"Okay," she said. She seemed curious, too.

With a two-handed tear, he opened up the bird and its stuffing was green, entirely green: hundred-dollar bills.

"Uncle Dick . . ."

"This is yours. He wanted you to have it."

"It's so much. . . ."

"If I'm not mistaken, it's fifty thousand dollars, and we'll get it into a college fund for you, right away."

". . . Is that from Mr. Kingman?"

"Yes, Becky."

"He wasn't such a bad man, was he, Uncle Dick? Looking out for me like this. . . ."

Stone nodded, and hugged her again, the bird full of money between them, the bills crackling like fall leaves.

He was grateful to the late gangster, whether a reincarnation or just a figment of this child's imagination; but he didn't see Moe as such noble guy.

Like the gangster had said, sending this kid to college was the best way for King Moe to look out for himself.